Chapter 1

It was dark now. He like⋯
senses came alive and the sh⋯
their outstretched arms, beckoning ⋯
would only see fear and foreboding. The town had finally
begun to bed-down, the hour being three thirty am, where
only the bar workers scurried home after another shift in
the seedy establishments that the town thrived upon yet
tried so hard to ignore. The homeless shrank back into the
doorways of high street shops long ago closed, symbolic
of the people who had been let down when the chain that
they worked at closed the doors and said goodbye.

Somebody else was out this cold November night beside
those that called the town theirs at this hour. These
people were the ones that he knew. He hadn't known
them well up until three weeks ago, but since that moment
when they hit his radar, he'd made it his business to know
them *very* well.

He knew all their names, ridiculous middle ones, their
families' names, their ages, their pet's names, their likes,
their dislikes, their favourite food, their habits, their
routines and their secrets. There in lay the reason he had
grown to know so much about them, their secrets. Or
rather a secret. A secret shared by all four of them.

8

In his experience a secret that is shared by four will always cease to be a secret. It is just the way us humans work. One person struggles to keep a secret, they feel the need to share, to be acknowledged or the burden becomes too much. Two people will become suspicious of each other, knowing what it's like to be a solo secret keeper – *have they shared the secret beyond me? Do I trust this one person? Maybe I need to share and have an ally in case they betray me.* With three people the group feels a certain trust. There is enough of you to be able to share the knowledge and feel that anymore would be a crowd. You three are the keepers of the secret, the privy three, where each has their strengths and together you are strong, like a proverbial triangle.

But four. This is the worst number. When there are four, those that hold onto that secret start to relax over it. Four of us already know, so what's the harm in telling one more? Statistically one of the four stands a chance of being a moron. They could have a drink problem. A drug problem. Perhaps they just have loose lips and were a poor choice to involve them in a secret. Whatever the case, he knew that four was too many. In this case it was *definitely* too many.

Men are so predictable. Pick the single one who struggles to get a date. Hire a lady of the night to get him nice and drunk. Pretend she's interested in him. Make him feel like an attractive woman finds him a turn on. He will do anything to seal the deal. He'll say something to try and impress her, make him sound like the big man. Sure, he would embellish in an attempt to make him seem even

REPRISAL

Printed in the United Kingdom

First Printing, 2020

ISBN 979-8692510587

Anything is possible if you just want it enough.

Huge thanks to:

Barry Hayes

Rob Shaw

Nick Winter

Louise Butler

&

Jon Doolan (Editor)

more like the stud she'd made him feel, but ultimately, there will be enough truth in his story to get what is needed. And so this moron gave the woman what she needed. She in turn passed this on to him and he paid her what she really needed.

Job done.

At least, the first part of the job was done.

Part two was digging deeper, watching and planning. Playing the long game, letting them have a victory. Letting them get cocky or blasé. They always did. He banked on it in fact. That's where he was this damp, miserable night. He was playing the long game. He was watching. The split conscience battled away at him during this stage and if he was not mistaken, the immoral side became bigger and heavier with every one of these that he had a part in. At least that's why he figured one shoulder dropped lower than the other. The bad side – the immoral – only sat one side and it was dragging him down. But it was necessary. It all was.

Three thirty-three am. Go time. Right on cue. A grey van turned the corner onto Friar Street, driving slowly, wipers intermittently swiping drizzle from the windscreen. The occupants no doubt checking their surroundings for anything that seemed out of place. Anything that would unnerve them. Anything that would make them abort. If they spotted him, they'd definitely pull the plug, but he was well hidden. He had found a spot high up on the old steeple clad roof of the town hall. The hall sat on the corner of the road right where the pedestrian zone began. His field of view covered all possible angles. He could not have asked for a better spot. He could even clearly see the statue of the great Queen Victoria in all her unattractive glory at the entrance to the local park.

The van sidled up to the front of the cheap beer selling chain bar and switched off the lights and the engine. There it sat. Silent. Waiting. But not waiting for something to happen. Waiting to see if anything should happen that they hadn't planned for. After two minutes the rear doors of the small Citroen van opened and two men climbed out, heads turning left and right, scanning the scene. Seemingly satisfied, they shut the rear doors and crossed the street.

His camera picked all this up. He snapped away with his large military grade lens, being sure not to reflect any light off the mirrored glass that would give his position away. The two men had shied away from the balaclava look. These days it was just too obvious that you were up to no good. Instead they had tight black baseball caps pulled down low to cover as much of their faces as possible. This was so the high mounted CCTV cameras couldn't make out your faces if you refrained from looking too high up. But he had them. He had caught their faces alright. He'd snapped them in the reflection off the glass fronted betting shop they had passed. He let a smug grin spread across his face. Amateurs.

They reachcd the front door of the county court. Their destination. The taller of the two turned and gently leant against the large double timber doors. He looked so casual, like he had done this a million times. The shorter one sidled up to the left-hand door and produced a key. One small bribe of an under paid security worker and bam – no need to break shit. He slid the key into the lock and turned. The door opened and the suspicious looking duo pushed on through the doors.

He could hear the pre alarm of the security system. They had twenty seconds in which to silence the alarm. They did it in six. They were in. One bribe - two keys. Physical and electronic. The taller one stuck their head out of the opened door and beckoned to the van with a short sharp wave of his gloved hand. All clear. The doors of the van opened - the driver and the passenger climbed out. The driver went to the back of the van and pulled out what looked like black holdalls. He closed and locked the van doors behind him as they purposefully walked across the street to the court's front door. The passenger entered and the driver turned, took one last look around before passing through the open door and closing it behind them.

Stuffing the camera into his black technical backpack and slinging it over his shoulders, he grabbed the harpoon gun he had rigged for this purpose and aimed. He fired the harpoon across the street into the lift motor room wall atop the county court building. He saw the heavy-duty harpoon slam into the brick wall and take purchase there.

He gave the trailing line a brief tug and, satisfied, tied the other end to a window cleaners anchor point. Next, he pulled out an automatic rappel pulley and attached it to the line. Grasping the small handles either side of it he launched himself off the town hall roof and the mechanism kicked into life, zipping him across the street 12 metres up in the air. The two buildings were of equal height, so gravity played no part in his journey, but the little contraption he had acquired worked blindingly. Within seconds he was touching down on the court's roof and running towards the lift motor room access door.

He had prepped the door earlier and wrenched it open, near enough pulling it off its hinges and rushed through into the dark stairwell. He didn't need a torch – his night vision had been honed over years of night ops. The wooden stairs creaked and groaned under his weight as he hurdled down them two, three, four at a time. This far up the noise wasn't an issue. The men downstairs would still be going through the first few rooms, checking the way was clear. He had time. Thirty seconds more and he would be in position.

The air vent ducting hatch was propped open just like he had left it. He dropped the main backpack and grabbed the small pouch he'd left by the hatch. He had to be quick now, diving into the stainless-steel rectangular chute. He had 10 metres to crawl before he was set. 10 metres of the ducting moving with his weight. He prayed he had got his timing correct or the men would see it moving for sure. He couldn't hear any voices, but they would be quiet, and he was making some noise. He scrabbled along and reached the vent that looked down on the room he needed. There wasn't anyone in there and it was pitch black. Nailed it.

He slowed his breathing and opened the small pouch. There wasn't much room for manoeuvre in the duct, but he managed to get the small snake camera out and thread it to a point where he could poke it through the vent slats. He held off actually sticking it through just in case they noticed on their initial scan of the room.

KERRCHUNK!!

Suddenly the lights all blinked on in the room below him. Then the huge door slowly swung open. There were three of the four men standing there. One let out a whistle as the room came into his view.

"Holy shit," said another of the three.

"Yes, boys. We've hit the big one here alright," said the third. He was the man from the passenger seat of the van. Clearly the main man here. "Zippy, get the bags."

"Yes, boss," the man who whistled acknowledged and turned back out of the doorway just as the two others entered.

He already knew what was going to be in the room, but it was still impressive. £100 thousand pounds in notes was a sight to behold alright!

'Zippy' came back into the room holding the black holdalls. Each man took a bag and started stuffing cash into them. They worked in silence until 'Zippy' spoke again. "So, Jamie, what are you going…"

"Zippy, you fucking idiot! No names! Jesus fucking Christ man. I'm George. You got that? GEORGE!" shouted the non-leader burglar.

"S-S-S- Sorry George. I forgot, what with all the excitement and all…"

George turned to the boss "Should have brought Bungle in for this bit. He's not bright but he can at least remember names for fucks sake…"

The boss spoke. "Alright alright boys. Zippy, switch the fuck on, George – no fucking shouting! Now, let's get these bags out of here."

They finished stuffing the wads of cash into the bags and zipped them up.

"Anything else you want from in here Matthew?" George asked the boss.

"No. We have what we came for. Let's foxtrot oscar."

With that they all left the room and carefully closed the door behind them.

He had it all on video. Then he remembered his mistake. He'd left the zip line in place. "You stupid cunt…"

The race was on. He squirmed backwards, camera in his mouth so he could use his palms to push himself. "Shit. Shit. SHIT!"

He needed to get that wire down. He doubted three of the four would notice it, but the boss would undoubtedly see it. Alarm bells would ring.

He was out of the shaft and hurtling up the stairs.

Chapter 2

He had an hour to kill before he was due back at work. He should sleep. But he doesn't. Since it happened, he needed extraordinarily little sleep. An advantage you could say seeing as he had nocturnal activities to attend to. Still, everyone needs to stop and take a breath sometimes. This was his time. He sat on his worn brown leather sofa, large 'Adventures start with coffee and odd socks' mug filled to the brim with strong coffee with a dash of milk cradled in his calloused hands. The flat he lived in had very few items of luxury in it. His filter coffee machine was one of those things.

The one bedroom flat in what he guessed you would call the suburbs of Reading, had a bed and a lonesome 4 drawer unit with his limited supply of clothes inside. The living room consisted of the leather sofa, a coffee table and a shelf on the wall with one picture on it. The kitchen was as sparse as the rest of the place he begrudgingly called home. The coffee maker on one side along with a microwave and a kettle. The fridge hummed away noisily. He wasn't even sure if the cooker worked, but it was there. If he dwelled on it all too long, he would be sad. He used to like cooking; throwing ingredients together in often random fashion to create some, and he had to admit this, bloody good meals. But that was the past. Now it was hydrated noodles and salami. Everyday.

It was seven in the morning and the sun was just rising on another November day. The drizzle from the early hours now gone. It was surprisingly mild still, but he could tell that the weather was on the turn. Soon everyone would be wrapped up like they were heading to the Arctic.

He slurped at the coffee. Damn that was good. It was a new blend he had picked up from the Polish shop down the road. He did enjoy a good coffee.

He sat and stared at where he guessed there should be a television set, the night's events fresh in his mind. He played them back, seeing them as if they were a projected movie from the 20's, dancing awkwardly in their silence across the off-white walls of his living room. He reached out and patted the camera that sat next to him on the worn leather, making sure it was still there. That is where the pictures were. That is what would condemn those idiots to a very rough ride behind bars. But not yet though; first they owed him. They owed him big time.

He finished the coffee, being careful not to drink the few grains of Ethiopian Arabica that had passed through the filter and headed for the shower. He stood, forcing himself to endure the cold water. He had read somewhere that it was good for you to shower in cold water. He had read that it would, over time, harden you to the cold. If it was true, it was a slow process. He still hated the cold water, but it also helped focus his mind. To untangle the knots of rage, guilt and desperation. Iron them out. Use their respective powers to focus on what he had to do. Right now, that was going to work.

Roughly towelling himself dry, naked he leaned on the sink and stared at his reflection. The face wasn't as young and youthful as it once was. Hell, it didn't even feel as young and youthful. At six-foot two he was taller than average with thick set shoulders propping up a wide neck. His greying brown hair was trimmed short round the sides like he'd always been taught in the military. On top it was longer than he preferred, at the time of his last cut he'd relented and let the girl do whatever she wanted. Hair styles mattered little to him. His piercing green eyes stared back at him, noting the lines and the grey stubble forming on his chin.

No longer interested in what he saw in the mirror, he pulled on fresh underwear, faded blue jeans and a dark green polo shirt. It was his way of appearing to look smart. The old battered brown boots with the half done up laces completed the look. Satisfied, he grabbed his keys and left his sad home.

"Morning, boss," a cheery constable called Joseph greeted him as he pushed through the staff entrance.

"Roger," he nodded in acknowledgement. He always thought it was odd when people had surnames that could or maybe normally would, be first names. Roger Joseph. Weird.

"Gilham wants to see you as soon as you get in," Joseph added, pushing open the door his superior had just came through. "She looked real pissed."

"What's new eh?" He replied, playing the classic old skool cop who has little time for superior's role.

"Ha! You know it, boss. Have a good one."

Then Joseph was gone.

He carried on towards his office. The station was well overdue an overhaul. The place was as run down and miserable as his own flat. But he liked it that way. There was a new fad of sharing buildings with the fire brigade. He wasn't thrilled with the idea. Lazy shits. The locker room was a cacophony of noise at change of shift. Lots of bravado and dark humour. 'Course, it's not as loud and brash as it once was. Times change and so has the type of person the police recruit… at least in general anyway. He came from a different age, albeit the end of an age. When he joined there were lots of old timers who had seen all kinds of shit, mixed with testosterone fuelled ex squaddies, of which he was one. Now you had to have a sodding degree or some shit just to get through the door. Even with a qualification, they still found a way to pay you shit money until you'd got years under your belt. It wasn't a job he would join now.

The old call centre was full this morning. He vaguely recollected reading something about a cross border exercise or some play nice shit that he no time for. The evidence room was as quiet and as lonely as usual, manned by poor Rostron who had taken a knife in the back from some low life years ago. Rostron could walk but he had left street work long ago. Poor bastard.

He passed numerous dingy offices and the main squad room. He could see at the end of the main corridor that someone was being hustled into one of the cells. Was it a man or a woman? It was so fucking hard to tell these days. Some even claim that they are gender neutral. Non-binary even. What a load of cod shit. He shook his head in disbelief.

"Fucking idiots," he mumbled. His office was only one room down from the cells. Noisy arse place to work. But then, when you work for the Anti-Corruption Unit, it's what you expect. Although the initialism sounds dull, because, well, it's a boring British one and it's not as recognisable as the Hollywood version derived from the cops out in the states, it is just as hated. Why don't they just call it Internal Affairs and be done with it?

His door was already ajar. He never left it like that. Ever. Someone had been or was in his office. He cautiously nudged the laminated teak door fully open with his boot. The door swung inwards with a faint squeak. The room was empty. But someone had been in. He was sure of it. He strode into the office and kicked the door closed behind him. Looking around he could see that nothing was out of place, which did not take long seeing as it was as bare as his flat. This was not entirely his fault mind you.

The dawn of computers had rid office space of metal filing cabinets, with everything being stored on some super hard drive or server or something. He wasn't ofay with computers but knew enough to get what he needed from the system when he needed it.

The dingy walls had several old-fashioned cork pinboards with various notes on them and a few mug shots to boot. There was a safe in one corner and then there was his desk. On old green glass shaded bankers lamp sat on top along with his ageing computer. That was normally it. But not today. Today there was a brown case file, URGENT stamped across the front at a random angle.

"What have we here?" He asked the room.

Taking his high-backed office seat at the desk he flipped open the file. There were only three pieces of paper in it. The first detailed a case from twenty years ago. Bank robbery that went wrong. Three killed. Case unsolved.

The second was a fresh case from the previous week. A robbery in Middlesbrough. Four killed. Same cause of death in all four. The same as the case from twenty years previous.

The third page had one photo on it.

"Fuck," he breathed.

Chapter 3

Pulborough was a nothing town in the English Southern counties. Sitting near insignificant villages such as Billingshurst and Petworth, there was literally nothing going for it other than the Brooks which for all tense and purposes was just a flood plain. Nothing ever really happened there other than the odd bunch of scrotes causing minor drug related offences. Strangely there was a petrol station that sold high-end four-by-fours and a dealership that sold classic cars such as beautiful E-Type Jaguars.

In this garage worked Paul Stephenson, an ex-footballer who played in an era before the money got big and, like most ex-pros that didn't enter coaching or buy a pub, he needed to find another job. Here he was, not unhappy with his lot, but not exactly living it large either like some of his past teammates. In general, he enjoyed where he worked due to the interesting motors that came through the doors and the opportunity to take some of them out for a spin.

It was just another Wednesday morning, sipping tea and browsing classic car auction sites while he waited for a customer to come and pick up his refurbished Aston Martin. Some kid had scratched 'Wanker' into the bonnet. To be fair, after meeting Mr Manuel, the statement wasn't exactly unsubstantiated.

The garage owner's daughter, Polly, bustled around behind him getting ready for a Black Friday-esque sale they were staging that weekend. All the local well-off toffs from the area would be turning up in their red corduroys, trophy wives hanging off their arms looking to take advantage of the free sandwiches and Buck's Fizz. It is how the rich stayed rich he supposed.

Ah but Polly. Paul would never admit it, but he was in love. She was a few years younger than him, curly blonde hair and legs to die for. The boss had made it quite clear when he employed Paul that his daughter was completely off the table. No passes should be made at her whatsoever. So far Paul had obeyed this rule but there was clearly chemistry between the two of them. Mild flirting had crept into their daily life. She was single; he was now single after his wife of twenty years had buggered off to Spain to be with a guy who still played football and was obviously years younger than her and crucially him. It had hurt Paul at the time, but he had reasoned that nothing lasts forever. Bitch.

He was gently daydreaming about what it would be like to whisk Polly off her feet and make mad love to her on his desk when an ancient Porsche 911 pulled up on the forecourt. It didn't look like it was in bad nick but definitely not something they as a garage would be interested in. He left his sordid thoughts behind and stood ready to greet the driver. Two men got out of the car and walked purposefully towards the glass front doors of the sales office.

"Gentlemen, welcome. How may I help you?" Paul began, straightening his navy-blue suit jacket as he stood, his patter a rehearsed affair.

The driver spoke first. "Alright, mate. We're after a particular car." His voice was hoarse, and his attire was scruffy at best. Faded blue jeans and a long sleeve off-white T-shirt with a picture of a surfer carving a wave splashed on the front. The sleeves were tight against some impressively large biceps. The image on the front stretched where his chest was pushing to burst out. This man hit the gym and even at the age of, what, 47? he looked in good shape.

His buddy wore one of those peaked caps that reminded Paul of Dick Van Dyke in Mary Poppins. He was similarly dressed but wore a dark purple polo shirt instead. He wasn't muscular either. Lean though, like a runner.

Paul smiled, "Well, what car is it that you seek, Mr…?"

The muscular man chuckled "Call me Smudger. I seek a Rover SD1. In grey."

Paul was quite taken aback. "Well," he started "That is a ridiculous coincidence."

"Oh, why is that?"

Paul swore the man was smirking. "Well, one came in just a couple of days ago. We haven't even advertised it yet. It is hard to put a value on something like that. It's not your usual classic car…"

"Bloody great car in its day though son. You're my age. You must remember them?"

"Well of course. Back in the day I was chased by one or two of them when they were cop cars…"

Paul could feel Polly looking at him differently now. Why did he say that? Who was he trying to impress?

"Really?" Mr Smudger seem fairly impressed anyway. "Good lad. Wouldn't have thought you had it in you mate."

"Ahem. Well, you know, I wasn't always a salesman," he stuck out a hand. "I'm Paul by the way."

The man took it in a firm grip. "Smudger," he said. "Now, about that Rover."

"Yes. Of course. Polly? Do you have the keys to the Rover please?" Polly did not look happy. He hoped it wasn't to do with what he had just said about being chased by the police. Idiot.

She reached into the drawer of her desk and handed him the small bunch of keys. She didn't say a word but made eye contact with him as he took the keys. Her eyes shifted towards 'Smudger' and back again. She looked worried.

Paul gave her a reassuring smile and turned back to the two men. "If you'd like to follow me."

Paul led the way through the side door and headed to the car park out the back of the sales office. To the right were the garages where the mechanics would normally be, but they had all been sent on a maintenance course of some kind run by Jaguar, so it was quiet in there today. The Rover was parked under a car port lean-to, waiting to be inspected by the mechanics.

The other man spoke for the first time as they walked past a row of classic cars.

"Fucking hell. There is a few quid here... ah man! I always wanted one of these!" His voice was strangely high pitched, like he'd been kicked in the balls. The car he was excited about was a 1963 Split-screen convertible corvette.

"Is that a Daytona blue one?" High pitched asked.

"You know your 'Vette's I See," Paul half turned to say. He doubted the man had the 95k that he needed for the motor.

"Always dreamt of owning one..." the man trailed off, daydreaming.

"So, here it is gents." Paul enthusiastically waved an arm towards the huge old Rover. "It's a 1987, Twin..." He was interrupted by Smudger.

"Twin plenum 3.5 litre V8 Vitesse. Originally at least. The block has been modified to a 3.9 litre. Coachwork black and grey interior. Did a stint as a cop car. Immaculate."

This is very strange, Paul thought. "Err, well, yes. Yes, that's all correct. At least I think so anyway. The mechanics haven't determined to what size the block had been bored out to… how do you know all this might I ask?"

Smudger chuckled heartily which turned into a throaty hacking. After a good thirty seconds of awful sounding coughing, he apologised. "Sorry about that Paul. This car in fact used to belong to me."

"Really? And you want it back?"

Now it was the turn of his mate to chuckle. He had brought his attention back from the 'Vette to the conversation. Paul gave him a strange look.

"Nah mate," Smudger admitted. "I just want what's inside."

Now Paul was properly baffled.

"Keys?" Smudger said aggressively, his demeanour changing abruptly. He held his hand out, waiting.

Paul didn't know what to say. He just sheepishly handed them over.

"Muchos Grassy arse," Smudger said, taking the keys and unlocking the big old car.

Paul built up the courage to ask, "What's inside?"

High pitched man answered, "Never you fucking mind."

"Um. No need for that mate. Perhaps I'd better go call the boss…"

"You'll do no such thing," Smudger admonished. He turned back towards Paul... he could see the panic in his face. "Kammy. Tie him up."

"Do what?!" Paul almost screeched. The man called Kammy grabbed him by the back of his neck and pushed him towards the garages.

"You had to go and ruin it didn't you Paul?" Smudger said like a disappointed parent. We were having a nice little chat there and you had to go getting all stupid on us. I'm sorry, but Kammy will have to gag you as well."

"No, No…" Was all Paul could manage. He could feel the sweat building under his arms as he was roughly pushed towards the workshops. What the fuck was going on?!

Two minutes later he found himself cable tied to the stanchion of the car lift, Gaffer tape over his mouth to keep the gag in place. He was petrified. But more than that, he was scared for Polly.

Chapter 4

His mobile phone buzzed in his pocket shaking him out of his stupor. The photo in the file had stirred something he had been trying to keep under wraps. He could feel the beast rearing its ugly head. The phone continued to buzz. He pulled it out of his jeans pocket. The Chief. Bollocks. He'd forgotten.

"Morning Chief," he answered.

"Did you not get the message?" Chief Gilham asked impatiently.

"Yes Guv, sorry I…"

"Never mind. Did you get the file?"

"I'm looking at it right now."

"Good. My office. Now."

He didn't have time to answer; she had hung up on him. The boss could be brutally blunt sometimes, but she was always honest. He liked that, and it was one of the reasons he respected her. He closed the file, slipped into the empty drawer of his desk and headed out the door.

Chief Gilham's secretary, Ruth, waved him through, barely looking his way. He knocked on the door and entered without waiting for permission. The Chief was on the phone, but waved for him to sit down, which he dutifully did.

Chief Gilham had started at the bottom, pounding the streets and earning her stripes. They had worked together briefly before she went up the ranks and he moved over to the ACU. She was a good cop and had proved herself time and again to all that had questioned her. She had never felt the need to impress anyone, doing things the way she believed was right. It hadn't taken long for her to be noticed. Fair play to her, he thought. Still not even 50 yet, she carried herself with confidence that undoubtedly came easier when you are good looking in a simple way. Never one for excessive makeup or jewellery. She just had a timeless beauty without being knock your socks off stunning. Her dark brown hair was pinned up like Sean Young in Blade Runner with a large bulbous fringe. Her green eyes had a depth to them that hinted to a map of a million galaxies. At 5 foot 6 she wasn't tall or short and her black uniform sat just right, creases in all the right places.

She would not be impressed with his appearance.

She put her phone back down in its cradle and sat back, her elbows on the arms of her office chair. Her hands came together, and her fingers linked like the two sides of a zip. Neither one of them spoke. They silently studied each other.

He gave in first. Impatient. "Where did the photo come from?"

"Let's just get this out there first shall we. This is not your case. You will not be working on it – it's not your department for starters. This is just me keeping you in the loop."

"For old times' sake?"

"Is that a thing we have? No. It's a professional courtesy."

"It's more personal than that."

"To you, yes. That's why I've included you."

"I appreciate it."

"So, we're clear. This isn't your case."

"Yes."

"Ok," Gilham said, clearly more relaxed now that was out of the way. "I'll brief you with what I know."

He stayed sat back in his chair, stony-faced, hands on his lap.

"The robbery in Middlesbrough was only brought to our attention because of the unusual murder weapon."

"Are we looking for a human sized turtle who practices the art of being a ninja? I don't fancy heading down the sewers Guv…"

Gilham actually raised a smile "You're not the first and no doubt won't be the last to make some Ninja Turtle joke over this. Just remember; people are dead."

He nodded. "Guv."

The weapon involved in all the killings was unusual indeed. Grandiose even. It's not every day you come across someone brandishing a sai. The three-pronged weapon was mainly used as a training tool in modern day martial arts. Although pop culture glamorised its use, it was something that at least in Western Europe, hadn't been seen as a murder weapon. That was until 1997 when the weapon was used to kill three people in a bank robbery.

Gilham continued. "No other murders or reports of misuse involving a sai have been reported since that day in '97… until now. The incident in Middlesbrough was two days ago."

"You think they've been in jail, don't you? Done a stretch and now they're out killing again." He probed.

"That is one train of thought. Could be a copycat killer. Could be totally unrelated."

"So, what has the other picture got to do with all this?"

Gilham took a breath. "It was found at the scene."

He stayed silent. His mind was racing. He could feel Gilham studying him, looking for a reaction.

He remained stoic, "At the petrol station?"

"Yes," Gilham confirmed "At the robbery in Middlesbrough."

"Was it just laying around?" He asked incredulous yet sarcastic.

"No. It was found, neatly folded, in the breast pocket of one of the victims."

"But we don't think that it belonged to the victim."

"No. There were no prints on it at all. Whoever put it there took precautions. If it had belonged to the victim, they surely had no idea they were going to be caught in the middle of a robbery and so it is *highly* unlikely that they would have taken precautions like wearing gloves when handling the picture."

"So, we think the perp with the sai placed it there."

"Or at least it was one of the perps."

"How many?"

"Two."

"We know that how?"

"CCTV."

"Any chance of an I.D?"

"Not a chance in hell. They all wore masks."

"What kind of masks?"

Gilham let out an oddly loud chortle "Get this. Ninja turtle masks."

He had to admit that was amusing, despite the situation. Two perps. Twenty-year gap in crimes. Fondness for the sai. And then the picture.

"It's a message to me," he said, matter of fact.

"That's what we think too. But why?"

He studied his hands, turning them over and over, looking at the callouses and the old scars, picturing how he would use them if he ever caught the men to blame for all his heartache. He didn't look up when he said "I think I put this guy away twenty years ago for a crime unrelated to the sai murders. He had that," he pointed at the third picture, "done as revenge against me. Now he is out, picking up where he left off and taunting me. Playing a game." He raised his voice and slammed his fist down on Gilham's desk. "SON OF A BITCH!"

Gilham did not react. Just watched the emotions and thought processes wash over her detective. She felt for him, she really did, but she could not have him losing it now. He was going to be needed.

"I'm sorry this has been brought up again…"

"You think it's ever gone away?" He asked angrily, instantly regretting it.

She ignored the outburst "Like I said, I'm sorry, but this an actual lead. Something to work with. We have a theory, so now it's up to Evans and Millen to figure it all out."

"What?!" He was genuinely shocked

"I told you at the start. This isn't your case, neither is it your department."

"But..."

"No buts. I realise your... emotional involvement here. That does not however put you on the case. If Evans and Millen need your input, they will ask. Got it, Detective?"

He was struggling to keep his anger under wraps. Fuck Gilham. Fuck Evans and Millen. He would work this out, even if it wasn't as a cop. "Yes, Guv." He got up and looked at her with an 'anything else?' face.

"Dismissed, Detective," she said with a wave of her hand.

"Ma'am," he nodded, barely controlling his anger. He turned and walked out of the office. Ruth was still at her desk and didn't look up at him as he walked past. There was someone else sat waiting to go in and see the chief. He didn't recognise him so just continued on his way, anger coursing through his veins. He clenched and unclenched his hands as he walked, desperate to explode and *hit something*... or someone. Nobody better piss him off in the next ten minutes. He needed to get to the station gym and unleash on the punchbag.

The man watched the detective walk by. He noted the clenching hands, the killer stare, and the purposeful walk. He clocked the glance he was given and noticed the 'I don't know him' look as the detective passed. The man studied the detective as he walked away. He could see the tension across his shoulders. That man was struggling to control his rage.

"The chief will see you now," Ruth said, not looking up from her keyboard.

'Thank you," the man said, standing. He buttoned his suit jacket and walked through the chief's open door, which he closed behind him. Gilham looked up as he entered, leaning back in her chair.

'Is he going to be a problem?" the man asked Gilham.

"That's what you were meant to tell me," she replied.

"He looks like he's struggling."

"Of course he is for fuck's sake!"

"I would like to quest…"

"Hell no. That would not end well. We will just let him be for now. I know him. He will not let this go. I bet he'll get there before Evans and Millen."

"With all due respect, Chief, this man is a person of interest. I am here because of him. It is my duty to question him. With inter-agency relations at an all-time low, do you really think leaving him be is a wise play?" He was doing little to disguise his frustration.

"It's a calculated risk." She sighed, turning to gaze out of the window. "He was a good cop once. Respected. Now that he works for the Anti-Corruption-Unit, he's lost something…"

"I don't think that was the change in job role."

"You know what I mean. What happened to his family changed him, no doubt. But the ACU has made him into an arsehole."

"Or maybe working for the ACU means he doesn't need to have friends. He can be an arsehole, go rogue, grieve… Or stew in self-loathing, or anger or whatever it is he feels."

"Maybe," Gilham admitted "But he's still our best shot at this."

"I hope you're right Chief. I hope you're right."

Chapter 5

The oil and grease covered gag was making him nauseous, but he had not dared move or try and spit it out until he was sure the two men were gone. At least that was what he told himself. In reality he was frozen with fear, dragging himself back from the brink of almost pissing himself. He had thought he was much tougher than this, but when it came to the crunch he was just as weak as the next man. He hated himself for it but tried to reason through the ever-growing fog in his head that there was nothing he could have done. Then a thought hit him as the self-preservation reactions began to wear off in the realisation that he was probably safe now. What about Polly?! 'Oh God!' he thought, suddenly desperate to get free. Sweat had caused the gaffer tape to begin to loosen on his face. He used his dry tongue to work the oily cloth against the tape, slowly but surely working the last of stickiness away from his cheeks. The tape fell away on one side and he spat the cloth out of his mouth, desperately trying not to gag as he did so. Finally, it dropped to the floor and Paul frantically tried to muster some saliva into his parched mouth.

His wrists were sore from the cable ties that held them together, his arms behind him, linked around the stanchion of one of the car inspection lifts. He wriggled his numb backside and shuffled his feet to the point where he could push himself up into standing position. If there was one part of him that was still strong, it was his legs. All those years of football training served him well. He was able to shuffle around the stanchion like an embarrassed pole dancing novice. He found that there was a crude weld on one side of the metalwork. He began frantically rubbing the cable ties against the rough metal. It didn't take long before he could feel the plastic weakening at which point, he doubled his efforts, now desperate to go find Polly.

Suddenly the ties gave way, and his arms were free. Rubbing his sore wrists, he set off towards the main sales office at a half trot. The fear of the two men lingering with him despite his worry for Polly. The Porsche was gone so it must be safe now he reasoned. Yanking open the rear door to the office he rushed in "POLLY!" He shouted "Jesus, POLLY!" he shouted again, skidding into the main foyer where his desk stood.

Paul Stephenson just stood still, staring, the colour draining from his face and the tears forming instantly. The lower lashes of his shocked eyes couldn't hold the tears back, the salty drops streaming down over his cheek bones. He had found Polly… but he wished he hadn't.

Paul couldn't drag his horrified eyes away from the scene. He had never witnessed anything like it, not even in a movie. Polly was dead, that much was horrifically clear. She was pinned up against the back wall of the office, her right arm straight up above her head. Her hair was splayed out against the wall, stapled to the pinboard that was behind her. This kept her head from slumping and exposed the truly sickening reason for her death. The beautiful Polly no longer had a lovely slender neck that he had ached to kiss. Now it was split wide open, blood still oozing from the gaping hole. Her chest was covered in her own blood that was now pooling on the floor beneath her feet that was suspended an inch or two off the floor. Her whole body hung from that the right arm that reached up above her head. Her hand had been speared with something that dug into the wall and held her limp body like a piece of art in a gallery. That something was a sai. A fucking sai.

Paul managed to fumble around for a phone and called the police. "A fucking sai," was all he could manage.

The official smoking area sucked balls. It was always full of prissy cheap lawyers, overzealous plods and emotional wrecks and most of them wanted to make small talk. He despised small talk but sometimes he got the biggest leads in the smoking area. Loose lips sink stupid pricks he liked to say. He almost smiled. Almost. But today was not one that he could put up with idiots and their problems.

Today he had retreated to his own smoking area where he was free to think and could avoid any interference. The roof of the station was always quiet, and he had never seen another smoker up here although he was certain someone else did use it because there were always fresh fag butts on the roof, and he smoked cigars. At home or when he had time, he would toke on large Cubans, but he relied on the small cigarette sized cigars that came in a handy tin for when he was on duty.

He took a drag on one such smoke, looking out over the sprawling urban landscape of outer Reading. He could hear sirens in the background until the dull roar of a plane taking off from Heathrow diluted the cities sounds. He tilted his head back, looking up into the clear sky and blew out the blue tinted smoke.

"Fuuuuucccccckkk," he breathed. A simple curse that masked a complex mix of emotions and problems. He had to keep an eye on those fucktards who robbed the county court, figure out how to take them down without arousing suspicion.

But now the demons of the past had been laid out for all to see. He had something to focus on. He had someone taunting him, which meant there would be clues, there was a chance to finally punish those that had killed all that had been left of his family. He was going to rip out their throats. Simple. His cigar hung from his lips as he looked down at his flexing hands, imaging how it would feel…

His train of thought was interrupted by the ringing of his mobile phone. He slipped it out of the rear pocket of his jeans to see it was a Detective that he had trained before he joined the ACU.

"What can I do for you Sam?" He answered, trying to sound at least semi friendly.

Sam was straight to the point as usual "Thought you'd like to know. There's been a murder."

He exhaled slowly, trying to keep his cool "And what has that got to do with me Sam?"

Sam was quiet for a moment before saying "A sai was used, boss."

His mind raced at a million miles an hour "What makes you think that would interest..." He didn't get to finish his question.

"Boss, I know about the photo. I wanted to let you know because I know it's not your case, but you SHOULD know, ya feel me?"

"Yeah, Sam," his voiced strained "I feel you. Appreciate the heads-up man."

"Be careful." With that Sam hung up, leaving him to listen to the *beep beep* that signalled the end of the call before slowly lowering the phone to his waist. He held it there, waiting to see if it rang again. Would Gilham let him know? This would be a test of where he and her were with this case.

Five minutes passed, the last of the cigar burned out in his pinched fingers, momentarily burning him although he barely noticed. The phone did not ring. He was on his own.

He saw Evans and Millen head out to their car; Evans climb into the driver seat and Millen into the passenger's, slamming the doors and backing out of the space they were in, to the right of the staff car park. There was barely a sound as the Hybrid motor purred out of the gate and pulled away out of view.

He brought the mobile phone back into life and selected an app simply called 'Tracker.' Technology had changed policing. Mobile phones could be traced, tracked and searched in an effort to convict those that seek to break the law. Internal investigations were no different. Sure, he ideally needed permission to track his colleagues, but knowing where they were and what they were up to was his business and he liked to stay ahead of the game.

He scrolled down the list that popped up and selected Evans. A few seconds ticked by before a map of the UK zoomed into the South East, then Berkshire, Reading and finally down to a blue dot that signified Evans' phone.

"Gotcha," he whispered into the cool morning air. He headed back into the building and then out to his car.

Chapter 6

"We're rich!" exclaimed Zippy, tossing bank notes in the air like confetti.

The other three men looked at him with scorn. They'd had an idiot work with them before. He hadn't had any composure or brain cells either. Not like the three of them. They survived because they were street smart and they had training. If you don't have at least one of those things, then you are going to get caught. Fact. No doubt about it. Trouble is, the others couldn't afford for you to be caught by the fuzz... imagine how that would pan out?! No, not acceptable. That loose end had to be tied up before it got out of control. It was handy having a friend at the metal recycling plant – all kinds of things could be crushed.

Still, they had a new idiot – an idiot with contacts. Zippy wasn't bright but he could get them info that they could use. They had blooded him on the County Court job, but now it was over to him to supply the next target.

"You like all that do 'ya?" Matthew asked the still jubilant Zippy.

Zippy stopped chucking money around for a moment to look quizzically back at the three men.

"Aren't you man?!" he asked, incredulous.

"Sure, we are," piped up George "But it's not enough is it?"

"Enough for what?" Zippy asked, perplexed.

George looked down at the idiot who was knelt on the stacks of cash that they had piled up in the centre of the filthy room. The abandoned power plant hadn't been used for years and nobody ever came down here. "It's never enough, is it?"

"I don't get it?" Zippy said, defensively, now rising to his feet and clambering off the stash.

"Enough," growled Matthew "Is when I say it's enough. Stealing this kind of cash is like a drug. It's addictive and addictions eventually ruin you one way or another. This one will get you caught and banged up."

The other three stayed quiet. Humbled. They all knew Matthew was the boss and the brains. They were just happy to be along for the ride.

"Now, let's get this money hidden while the heat cools and then we can come back for it. Until then Zippy, it's now on you to find us the next job."

"Yes, boss," Zippy said keenly. "You can count on me."

"I hope so," Matthew replied with just enough menace in is voice. "I hope so."

There was no need to tail the car with Evans and Millen in and risk being seen. He didn't really have enough respect for the two detectives to seriously worry about them being aware enough to spot a tail, but why risk it? The tracker he put on their phones over a year ago would lead him to the right location anyway.

They had left the M4 motorway and were now heading south on the dreaded M25 towards Gatwick. The traffic was surprisingly light, but at 11am on a Wednesday you would expect a lull in the congestion the motorway was renowned for.

Questions whirled round his head. Was it someone he had locked up? He would have to go through his case files, which would take some time. That being said, very few of his cases would even remotely indicate anything of this magnitude or of this brutality. There was certainly no history of a sai being used. It was a weapon so unusual that it fascinated him. Where would you get one? Is it an indication of ethnicity? Has it been used with skill or just brute force?

None of it was adding up which was why he needed to see the crime scene. He wasn't on the case, but he suspected that Gilham was nudging him to follow his nose and get involved, even if she couldn't officially say it.

All of this was going on and he still had his investigation into three bent cops to take care of. Take care of and take advantage of.

The tracker app on his phone that was mounted on the dash bleeped, showing the car coming off at the next junction. Where were they going?

They joined the A3 heading towards Guildford and he settled back into his leather seat, his mind searching and cross referencing anything he could think of that might spark inspiration.

They had pulled into a multi-storey carpark close to the centre of Horsham which was a pretentious medium sized town in the heart of Sussex. Kammy put a ticket in the window of the Porsche and left it, duffle bags stuffed with the cash grasped in their hands. Going up a level they located the silver BMW estate and threw the bags in the back and slid into the old but luxurious seats. Smudger let Kammy drive this time, preferring to use the time to check messages on his phone. He had a hit list and he needed to get them done as soon as possible.

"Where to now, boss?" Kammy asked, selecting reverse on the auto box and backing out of the space.

"Head to Crawley mate. We need to get cleaned up. Kruszynski will sort us out"

Kammy didn't look happy. "Does it have to be him?"

Smudger laughed out loud, "Don't you worry Kammy, I'm sure he won't bully you!"

"I ain't worried... " He didn't bother finishing his sentence. There was no point. Smudger was laughing too loudly. He did not like being laughed at.

Eventually Smudger ceased his laughter which turned into another phlegm-filled coughing fit before calming down. He held his hands up to the light as the car purred out of the multi-storey and into daylight once again.

They were covered in that girl's blood. He smiled. Kammy had pulled a hoodie over his polo shirt to cover the blood from where he had held the girl up. Messy job but boy was it fun. Would have been nice to spend more time on her – she was pretty hot after all – but it wasn't the time or the place. There were things that needed to be done and he needed a new sai.

The blue dot had stopped moving so he pulled his 1990's Rover coupe into a supermarket and found a vacant spot at the back of the small carpark. He left the engine running and buzzed his window down. He continued to stare at the screen on his mobile and lit another cigar. He didn't like to smoke in his car when it wasn't moving as it made the car stink without the venturi effect of the passing wind to suck the blue smoke out and away, but his mind was focused on that blue dot and what was going to come next.

Two minutes passed and the dot hadn't moved. It was a mere 200 yards away and he had not seen any traffic lights or signs indicating roadworks up ahead, so they must have stopped. They could have been involved in an accident which would explain the unmoving dot, but he could see the road from his parking space and the traffic was still moving. They must have come to the crime scene. Time to go play.

He found himself pulling into a classic car garage that was jam packed with police cars. They were not the Thames Valley ones he was used to seeing, as they were now in the jurisdiction of Sussex police. He pulled up behind Evans and Millen's car which was parked along with various other nondescript boring cars that had to belong to other detectives. He got out and approached the blue and white police tape where a throng of journalists were gathered. He caught the attention of the bobby who was tasked with keeping them at bay.

"Can I help you sir?" The young Hispanic bobby asked, eyebrows raised.

He pulled his badge out of the back pocket of his jeans and flashed it at the young cop. "ACU."

The young cop looked a bit confused "Sorry, Guv, but that's not one of our badges… "

"Bang on son," he nodded "But a police badge nonetheless. I'm here to help the two detectives that have just arrived."

The cop looked a little uncertain but nodded and lifted the tape for him to pass under. "Your colleagues went round the back there," he said, pointing towards the back of what looked like the main sales office.

"Thank you… "

"Saunders, Sir."

"Carry on, Saunders."

"Sir," he said, bobbing his head slightly out of respect for rank.

He idly wandered round to the back of the building, so far amazed and appalled at how easy it was to just waltz into a crime scene. They really should have had him sign in. Where was the log? Surely Saunders isn't the only security they have here? Not that it bothered him. Made his life easier after all.

He turned the corner of the main building and found himself looking at the workshops for the garage. He spotted several classic cars including a split screen

51

convertible Corvette. Gorgeous. He made a note to take a closer look before he left.

A group of men walked out of the right-hand workshop as he turned towards them. He spotted the tall Evans straight away, who in turn saw him and locked him with a stare. He simply nodded and gazed back at him. He saw Millen follow his partner's stare and saw him raise his eyebrows. Both cops were in their mid- forties with enough experience under their belts to be respected around the station. Both dressed smartly, Evans in a blazer and jeans while the shorter Millen wore a slightly more relaxed fitted navy blue jacket. The kind you see outdoor enthusiasts sporting. The kind that look like shiny duvets.

The two detectives made their excuses with the group and marched over to him.

"What the fuck are you doing here?" Millen started, jabbing a finger in his direction. He appeared to have collected a lot more grey hair since they'd last crossed paths.

Evans jumped on board now "Are you fucking kidding me? Investigating US?!"

Millen again "You've got some nerve. We're not even on our patch! Who told you we were here?" The anger and indignation rising in his voice.

Evans again "My partner asked you a question; What the fuck are you doing here?"

"Gentleman," he said calmly. "I am not here for you although you doth protest vigorously even without a word from me. A guilty conscience perhaps?"

"Don't you even… " Millen seethed

He interrupted the detective. "Rest assured, gents, you are not part of any ongoing investigation. In fact, I wasn't even here for a police related reason."

Evans calmed down a bit now and even seemed to shrink a little. His anger had made his six-foot five frame seem even larger. "What are you doing here then?"

"I came down to see a car although I seem to have found a crime scene, no… ?"

"What car?"

"A Rover. You know I drive a Rover already, right? Heard there was a classic here… "

Millen and Evans looked at each other. Evans spoke again "A Rover SD1?"

He nodded keenly like a car enthusiast would, "Yeah, that's the one! Is it true? Do they have one?"

Again, Millen and Evans exchanged looks. Millen spoke this time. "Look, this seems like a ridiculous coincidence… or *something,* and bearing mind your link to this case… Come with us"

Evans grabbed his partner's arm, "You sure about this, Keith?"

"Yeah, buddy. The chief said he might turn up. Let's just get on with it."

Evans let his partner go and shrugged. "Come with us," he gestured by a wave of the hand.

The three of them walked through a freshly glossed green wooden door into the main building to a throng of SOCOs, detectives, coroners and paramedics.

"Shit boys," he whistled, keeping up the act of innocence, "What happened in here?" The two of them ignored him but everyone else turned to see who was being so vulgar. He mock waved to the room in response.

A woman in a grey two-piece suit came marching over to the three of them. "Gentlemen. Can I *help you?*" She had a Welsh accent, strong but not rural. From one of the big cities he presumed. Her blonde hair was pulled back into a simple ponytail, leaving a small fringe covering her forehead. She wore little in the way of makeup, preferring to keep her image professional he guessed. Simple yet efficient. She might be a pain in the arse.

"Sorry, ma'am. We are the detectives from TVP. Evans and Millen," Evans said with a hint of fear.

"Yes, I heard you were coming. You're working a on a case that has links to this MO?"

"That's correct, ma'am," Evans confirmed.

"And who might you be?" She asked him directly with no tact evident in her voice.

He smiled. "Quinn, ma'am, ACU. Also TVP." He offered out a hand for shaking.

She looked at him with as much distrust as any cop seemed to. She took his proffered hand anyway. Strong grip.

"And why might you be here, pray tell?"

Millen butted in before he could answer. "Ma'am, he's not on this case. It seems he was here for a car. A coincidence. But as it happens, he does have a link of sorts to the case. More specifically the MO."

She'd held his gaze throughout Millen's explanation. "You concur with that statement? She asked Quinn directly.

"To be honest, ma'am, I don't know what the MO is. I just came down to view a Rover."

That grabbed her attention. She glanced across at Evans, who nodded back at her. "A Rover you say?"

"Yeah, why is everyone being funny about that?" he feigned innocence. In reality he had spotted the blue police tape cordoning off what he knew was a SD1, even though he had only seen a rear quarter panel. What he didn't know was *why* it was cordoned off.

The detective seemed to make a decision right there and then. "Very well. This all seems a little odd if I am honest but colour me intrigued. I'm Detective Tabb and I'm in charge of this investigation. I'm not sure what link you have to the MO or if your presence here is in fact coincidence, but I'll take any help I can. This way gentlemen." She turned and led them through the throng of people and presented them with the crime scene.

"Holy shit," breathed Millen.

"Messy, right?" Tabb asked matter of fact. "The MO?" she asked him. No messing around with her.

"Yeah, as it happens, the MO is… how do I put this? Relevant."

"Relevant?" Tabb almost spat. "Relevant? To what?"

"It's the murder weapon, ma'am. The sai."

Tabb went quiet. "I want to know what's going on here and I want to know NOW."

Chapter 7

The two up, two down council house looked exactly that. A council house rammed in between other council houses. Smudger never could understand why Kruszynski lived here. He had earned enough money over the years supplying weapons to the underbelly of society that he could live wherever he wanted. Kammy knocked on the plastic door, preferring a knock to the shrill chime of a doorbell. A few seconds passed before the door was gently opened by a young girl they didn't know. She had what appeared to be a hastily thrown on pink satin nightgown even though it was lunchtime. Her bright red lipstick was half smeared across her left cheek and her heavily mascaraed eyes looked puffy and bloodshot.

"Help you?" she asked bluntly, here thick Eastern European accent plain to hear.

"You are…?" Smudger cooed, reaching out to touch her hand that was gripping the nightgown together at the front like a giant hair clip.

She recoiled, anger flaring in her face, "The fuck are you?!" She spat

Smudger laughed, "Let us in, Wench," he said, pushing his way into the entrance way. She fought to push him back, letting go of her robe in an effort to stop him. Her ample breasts were suddenly on show to anyone who might pass.

Anyone that did see this scene would also note, as Kammy did, that they were still in the right place. "Detsi!!" She screamed

"What the fuck is going on out here?" Came a booming German voice accompanied by heavy footfalls on the creaky stairs. Smudger backed off and stepped back outside.

A giant man with an enormous beard appeared behind the girl who was now trying to cover her chest back up. She scowled at Kammy who was mouthing 'Nice tits' at her from behind Smudger.

The girl started jabbering in Polish and pointing her figure at the two men on her doorstep. The large man stood there in the doorway, blocking the whole thing. Roughly 50 years old and showing signs of a once impressive frame giving way to gravity, he cut an imposing figure. He stood in only his boxer shorts, a large bulge evident, arms crossed over what appeared to be a tattoo of a Swastika.

When the girl finally stopped jabbering on there was silence. Then the large man started laughing. A loud, booming laugh that Smudger could have sworn he could feel pounding through his chest. He smiled.

"Smudger!" The man boomed, his laughter ending as he thrust out a hand the size of a leg of lamb.

"You are out, yes?" He asked, his thick Austrian accent less refined than the great Austrian oak he resembled.

Smudger grinned and took the large hand "Well, if I'm not out, I really shouldn't be here should I?!"

The Austrian boomed a laugh again even if the comment wasn't that funny. "I am pleased to see you. Come in," he said, letting go of Smudger's hand and waving them through. They dutifully followed the man through to the small dark living room. "Please, take seat," He gestured at a cream leather sofa that faced an enormous flatscreen television. "Woman," he added, "get us beers." He took a seat in a giant tartan smoking chair with high wings. It suited him.

They could hear the grumblings of the girl, the sound of the fridge opening and the clink of beers bottles coming together. She padded across the luxurious carpet and handed a beer to each man, Detsi last. She turned to leave, grumbling still and fixing Kammy with a stare. She was soon snapped out of it when one of Detsi's huge hands slapped her on the butt, making her yelp. "Leave us," he said, flatly. She scurried off and away up the stairs.

The three men twisted the beer caps off and toasted the air to each other before taking a swig.

"So, what brings you to my door?" Detsi asked, leaning back in the great chair.

Smudger pretended to study the label on the bottle as he spoke "I'm collecting it all."

Detsi looked surprised. "All of it?"

Kammy spoke up now, "Yeah all of it."

Detsi Kruszynski suddenly leaned forward, balling his spare hand into a fist "Who told you to talk?" He barked at Kammy who shrank back in fear. Then Detsi laughed "You always so easy to scare, Kammy."

Smudger grinned and slapped Kammy reassuringly on the leg. "As Kammy here said, yeah, all of it."

Detsi slumped back in his chair again. "Retiring with your money?"

"Something like that, yeah. I have something to take care of first."

"What do you need?"

"Just to clean up," Smudger said, showing the big man the blood on his hands "And some of my chosen weapon."

Detsi nodded. "Bathroom upstairs on the left. Kick her out if she is in there. The other thing? I need an hour."

"You're the man, Detsi," Smudger said, raising his bottle in acknowledgement at the huge man who returned the gestures. The two men took large swigs of their beers while Kammy sat back meekly, nursing his beer between his hands.

The small sales office was bustling with Sussex Police and in the centre of it all stood a weary internal affairs cop from another force who had no real right to be there. "It's not pretty, is it?" he said, stating the obvious.

"That's one way of putting it I suppose" Tabb acknowledged.

He took a step closer to the poor girl hanging on the wall by her impaled hand. "Can I trust you, Tabb?" he said, his voice emotionless.

"'Can *I* trust *you?'* is the question I should be asking, Detective Quinn. You don't even belong on this crime scene. Give me one good reason to let you stay." The anger in her voice clear for all to hear. The others in the room had come to a hushed silence, sensing something was going on.

He continued to look at the girl on the wall like she was art in a gallery. "You want to know about the sai?" He asked, his back still to Tabb.

Tabb looked across at Millen and Evans who nodded back at her. "Very well. I'm not happy with this but my gut is telling me to listen to you," she growled. She turned to the rest of the room. "Everyone out! Take a coffee break."

The room slowly emptied, the only sounds to be heard were those of latex gloves being removed and the shuffling of feet. When the last person left, she spoke again, "Well, gentlemen. Wow me."

He remained with his back to the three cops, analysing the girl. "How'd she get so high up?" He asked the room.

Tabb replied, "We're working on the assailant being somewhere around the six-foot five mark based on the height of that sai and the information given by the witness."

That made him turn around to face the other three "Witness?"

"Well, he's seen the men but was tied up when they *actually* did this," she shrugged, waving a hand in the direction of the girl. "Out in the workshops. He's pretty shook up."

"I don't doubt that," he agreed, turning back to the girl. "But look how high up she is. Both men would have to be over six feet five to be able to hold the body up and then place the sai. Did the witness say how tall the other perp was?"

Tabb remained silent for a moment and then sheepishly said "He did… and no, they weren't tall. Less than six feet."

He began widening his analysis of the scene. "There were just the two of them?" He asked.

"Yes, just two. Tell me about the sai…"

He remained silent, scouring the scene. The rest of the room looked untouched like there had been no discernible struggle with the girl. It looked too perfect in fact. "Anyone else think the room looks a little too neat considering what we have here?"

Evans spoke up "I've got to say that struck me. All the chairs are tucked away neatly, there's no paperwork on the floor, spilled coffee…nothing out of place."

"Exactly," he nodded in agreement "Like it's been tidied up after the murder."

"What are you saying?" asked Tabb.

"The SOCOs have been concentrating on the girl and the immediate area, thinking the rest of the room is unaffected. But they got her up there somehow didn't they? They must have stood on something?"

All four of them immediately started looking around the sales office. There wasn't a huge amount to look through that might have been used as a makeshift stool. It was Millen who found it.

"Ma'am. I think this is a small print…" The other three gathered around. Sure enough there was a faint print of a boot on the upholstery on a chair. It was one of the ones set out for a client to use when negotiating the sales of a car. It had static legs so wouldn't have swivelled when stood on and had been oddly tucked under the desk where a seat for a client would have been pulled out, inviting a customer to sit and be comfortable, ready to part with cash.

"Good work," Tabb acknowledged Millen. "I'll get that analysed. But where did the blood come from? The blood on the floor is an untouched pool."

He took a cigar out of its small tin and placed it behind his right ear. "Yes, I did wonder that, but that cut must have meant blood spurted out initially. From the angle of the cut across the neck, the murderer must have been almost directly in front of her, meaning most of the blood would have splattered over them. Any spray that went elsewhere I assume was hastily cleaned up…"

Millen again, "But why?"

"Why tidy the scene at all?" he countered. "I'm guessing that there will be smudges of blood on the floor where it's been hastily wiped if you use UV."

"To cover the footprints," Tabb agreed, nodding.

"Exactly."

Tabb played it out as they worked the scene. "Ok, so one man to stand on the chair, holding the body up against the wall… Are we saying she was alive when placed up there?"

"Judging by the faint bruise on her left cheekbone I'd say she was punched and knocked at least semi unconscious before they attempted to get her up there. The body had enough time to start the bruising before it was drained of blood and the bruise never took hold properly."

"And we can assume," Evans chided in, "that one of the assailants is left-handed."

"*Yes* Evans," he said, impressed.

Back to Tabb. "Ok, girl punched, chair moved. One stands on the chair holding the girl up against the wall while the other... not on a chair? Grabs her arm and impales her hand with the sai..." She looked at the other three for confirmation.

"How tall are you Evans?" Quinn asked the scowling detective.

"Six three," Evans replied.

"Could you have placed that sai there without standing on anything?"

Evans seemed to try and answer by looking at the scene from a distance before realising he would have to get close to the corpse. He went over and mimed stabbing the girl's hand with an over arm motion, way over his head. He arced his arm back and forward in a stabbing motion. "I don't think so," he said, still arcing is arm through the supposed movement.

"And if you were two inches taller?" He nudged.

Evans continued to ark his arm over and over. "Yeah, I think so. Yeah. But it would be at the limit of my reach for an ark like that. I'd have to be strong to be able to get the sai through the hand and into the wall when at the limit of my movement though."

He rubbed his chin in thought, absently flicking the throw away lighter in his pocket. "Does that match the description given by the witness?"

Tabb Answered "Yeah. Tall, muscular… but not overly big. Looked like he had been a gym rat at some point. Late forties. And that brings us to the sai and the reason you're even in this room."

He breathed out slowly before saying "Nineteen years ago my brother, his wife and my nephew were murdered."

Tabb looked genuine when she said, "I'm so sorry."

He nodded his appreciation. "We never caught the murderer. Kitchen knife. We've had no leads at all. That was until this morning."

"What happened this morning?" Tabb urged him to go on.

It was Millen who took up the story, "There were murders in Middlesbrough two days ago. Four killed in a robbery. The murder weapon was a sai."

"I don't see the correlation with your family's case…?" Tabb admitted.

Quinn spoke softly "That's because there wasn't anything to link them. Not until the scene was searched. They found a picture stuffed into one of the deceased pockets. The picture was of my dead family. It was a picture we'd never seen before. This picture was different. The picture showed something that wasn't there before. Something that wasn't at the scene when we arrived. There was a sai on top of the kitchen work top."

"Shit," Tabb breathed.

The room fell silent.

He spoke first, "Have you checked her skirt pocket?"

Tabb shook her head and walked over to the girl, pulling on a latex glove. She gently slipped her fingers into the small pocket on the side of the skirt and pulled out a small piece of folded paper.

The room was deadly silent. She took the few paces back to meet the others. She carefully opened up the piece of paper on the desk. It was a computer printout of a photo on A4 white paper. He moved away as soon as he had seen the photo. It was a close-up of his sister in law. Head and shoulders. She was still alive at this point. Pleading with her eyes to be let go. Sadly, you could also see the resignation that she was going to die in them. Her ginger tinged hair was theatrically splayed out like a spider's web from her scalp.

"Her hair," Tabb murmured. "It's like the girl here."

Underneath the picture were hastily written words. 'Watcha gonna do?'

"That's aimed at you," Millen said, even managing to sound sorry.

"Yep. I would say so, Millen. It's ink from a pen rather than a printout though, right?"

"Correct," Millen confirmed

Tabb jumped on it. "I'll get all the pens here analysed for prints."

"You never know I guess," Quinn said, trying to sound optimistic.

"What I don't get is how all of this links together?" Tabb asked the room.

A brief silence ensued before he spoke again. "The theory is that in '97, before I was ACU, I arrested a guy for a crime unrelated to the robberies come murders. Yet it seems clear that he was probably guilty of the ones in '97 involving the sai. As revenge for being put away he killed my family. Fast forward twenty years and I'm guessing he's been released from prison and what's he gone and done? The job in Middlesbrough. From there he's hit this place. But why here?"

Tabb rolled all that over in her mind before speaking. "If this is the guy who did the job in '97 and in Middlesbrough and you say he was banged up in between, how could he have killed your family...? I'm sorry, that was insensitive..."

"It's ok," he reassured her, "He must have ordered the hit. Maybe the guy who is with him now did it. Maybe it was someone else completely. Either way he's taunting me. Like he wants to be caught. But caught by me."

Evans spoke up, "You're saying he wants to go back to prison?"

He shook his head, "No. I think he wants to face off against me. He's punished me emotionally for 19 years. Now he wants to hurt me physically."

"Sounds like you're jumping to conclusions there..."

"Maybe I am," he admitted, "But it's what I'm working on."

Tabb interjected, "But you're not on this case."

"I think you can see that I'm involved whether you or my Chief like it or not."

Tabb stayed quiet.

"So, why here?" He asked again, hoping to turn the conversation away from him.

Tabb and Evans spoke in unison. "The car."

Chapter 8

There was a knock at the door and this time Detsi answered it now that he had put some clothes. Kammy and Smudger looked at each other, eyebrows raised. Prison had been tough and weird at times, but this house was out there weird. It was the third knock at the door since they had been there.

The first visitor was a woman with a gym bag stuffed with clothes for them to change into. The old blood-stained ones were shoved back into said bag and the woman disappeared with it. Detsi assured them that they would be disposed of. No problem.

The second knock at the door had been two men dressed in goth attire, noses pierced through with rings, tattoos up their necks and hair that looked as though it hadn't seen shampoo in years. These two men walked into the living room where Kammy and Smudger sat and emptied the contents of a large carboard box onto the floor and then promptly left without saying a word. They dumped a snake onto the floor. A fucking huge snake.

"What the fuck, man!" Kammy squealed, recoiling his legs up onto the sofa.

"Get your feet off the leather, dickhead!" Detsi shouted. When Detsi shouted, Kammy obliged, even if it was somewhat sheepishly.

"Detsi," Smudger chuckled "What the hell is that doing in your living room?"

"It is my pet, Ashley."

"*Ashley?!*" Smudger exclaimed. "What kind of name is that for a snake?"

Detsi seemed offended, "It is a Python. Ashley is a good name, no? He has been to the vet. He was not eating. Poor thing." Detsi gathered the huge snake in his arms and carried it away upstairs.

"This is a fucking odd house," Kammy mumbled. "Can we go?"

"Get a grip Kammy. We'll be gone shortly. I just need my sais," soothed Smudger

"I hope they bloody hurry up."

"They'll be here. Focus on our next job will ya? It's the Volvo next."

Kammy pulled out his phone. "It's not far away is it?"

"It's up in Berkshire somewhere."

"It's in a shithole. Slough. About an hour and a half from here."

That's when the third knock at the door came.

"Here you are Smudger," Detsi proclaimed, holding a leather satchel in his massive hand, "Your delivery."

Smudger stood and accepted the package. He laid it on the small pine table in the corner of the room and slowly unzipped the case that ran around the edge. Inside were six gleaming silver sais with blue cord wrapped around the handle. He picked one out and examined it. "Beautiful," he said, impressed, "It'll be a shame to leave them behind."

"What do you mean, leave them?" Detsi asked, confused.

"They are all part of a trail for someone. They will all be left bar one. That one I will use on him."

Detsi merely shook his head. "I do not understand you English."

"And I don't understand you my friend. How much do I owe you?"

"It is a freedom gift."

Smudger nodded his thanks. "I appreciate it Detsi, I really do. Now, we'll be out of your way. Thank you, again old friend. Come on Kammy." He packed the leather satchel back up with the silver weapons.

Detsi and Smudger shook hands while Kammy scurried out the door. "Take care big man," Smudger added.

"You no worry," Detsi boomed. "I go finish woman off now."

With that he closed the door and the two men headed back to the BMW. Kammy got in the driver's seat again.

"Let's get some grub on the way, shall we?" Smudger asked rhetorically.

"Yeah, boss, I'm famished."

Tabb led them out to the Rover. "Here it is," She said in way of introduction. "Were you really here to look at this?" She asked him, somewhat doubtful.

Quinn just gave her a wry smirk in response. "A classic motor for sure. Although it looks like the interior has been messed up," he said, peering inside the big old car. "Was it already like this?"

Millen brought him up to speed. "No. The witness, a salesman here by the name of Stephenson, said the two men arrived in an old Porsche and asked to see the car. He said that it was weird as the car had only just come in and they hadn't advertised it as yet. When he introduced the car to them, the one known as Smudger told him information about the car that even he didn't know."

"It used to belong to him?"

Millen nodded "That's what he told the witness. We're checking with the DVLA for previous owners' details."

"Good. Although that seems a little too easy doesn't it?"

"Agreed," Tabb joined in. "It can't be *that* easy, surely."

Millen shrugged and continued. "Smudger said he just wanted what was inside and then had the other guy, by the name of Kammy, tie him up in there." He pointed to the workshop.

Quinn looked to where Millen was pointing and then returned his attention to the Rover. "The upholstery of the rear seats has been ripped up… No, ripped open. Whatever they wanted must have been stashed inside the seats. Money? Drugs?"

"The sniffer dog is on his way. We'll be able to tell after that," Tabb confirmed.

"Ok," he said, standing straight again. "The two names. They don't ring any bells with me. If they are their real names, we can assume that Smudger is a Smith. If the DVLA come back with anything it could lead to a trail of cars that they've owned. Perhaps there are more cars with stuff stashed inside."

Evans broke into the conversation. "If they have been locked up for twenty years, they could be out collecting everything they'd stashed before they got caught. The cases we know about were for cash so I'm guessing it was cash stuffed in the seats."

Everyone went quiet as they mulled this over. Quinn spoke first. "I agree with you, Evans. Probably cash. What we can assume is that there are more stashes and there will be more taunts towards me. Based on past history here, I'd be worried about more murders too."

Tabb looked angry. "Fuck," she cursed. "Sussex and TVP will have to keep working together on this. Evans, Millen, I'll set up a task force and include you. I'll clear it with your Chief. Can you update Gayle and Henry?"

"Sure thing," Evans agreed. The two detectives walked off to find their Sussex counterparts.

That left Quinn with Tabb. She spoke first. "I am genuinely sorry about all this. Perhaps though it could bring closure on what happened to you. Until then I think you should be assigned to this case even if you have emotional links to it."

"I appreciate the sentiment, Tabb, but my Chief will never sign it off. She knows I'll pursue the case anyway though." He pulled out a business card and handed it to Tabb. "I'd appreciate being kept in the loop though."

She took the card and said, "As long as *you* keep *me* in the loop!"

"Good luck, Detective," he said before walking back off to his car.

Tabb watched him walk away. She could feel that there was something just not right about that ACU agent. He was clearly a good cop with an eye for detail... but something bothered her about him in equal measures as she felt sorry for him. She made a mental note to look up his file.

He didn't head straight for his car. An ambulance was still parked up out the front of the garage. He knocked on the rear door and a young female paramedic opened the door. "Can I help you?" she asked sweetly.

"Yes, do you still have Mr Stephenson in there?"

"We do, yes. Who are you?"

"May I have a word?" He asked, flashing his badge at her.

"Ummm, I guess so," she said, opening the door wider so he could climb aboard the ambulance. "But I must warn you that I will not tolerate any questions that may cause further undue stress."

Stephenson was sat up on the bed. There was clearly nothing physically wrong with the man bar some sore wrists from where he had been tied up.

"Mr Stephenson, I'm with Thames Valley Police. I only have one question for you if you don't mind?"

Paul looked back at him, clearly still in shock. "Sure."

"Thanks, Mr Stephenson..."

"Paul."

"Sorry, Paul. Did you try and stop the two men? Did you try and fight them?"

Paul Stephenson immediately broke down in tears. The Paramedic rushed to his side to comfort him, throwing an accusatory glare at Quinn.

He just grimaced and left with one parting word that was said loud enough so that Stephenson could hear. "Pathetic."

He could hear the gasps of shock from the paramedic, but he didn't care. He left the man sobbing and got back into his car, lit the cigar he'd stashed behind his ear earlier and drove off. He had an appointment.

"You have to be fucking kidding me," shouted an outraged Chief Inspector Gilham. "From the council offices?!"

"Yes, ma'am. That's correct," confirmed a sheepish Constable Roger Joseph. He wanted the ground to swallow him up. How did he end up delivering this bad news to the Chief? Surely it was a job for at least a Sergeant? That slippery snake Sergeant Hogan should have been stood here. But here he was confirming that 150 grand had been stolen from the council offices last night.

"Christ, I'm gonna get all kinds of crap for this," she said, now pacing her office floor, hands behind her back. "Who's assigned to this?"

"Nobody as yet, ma'am. Sergeant Hogan hasn't given it to anyone. Thought you'd like to know first…"

"Hmmm. Not a fan of that Hogan. Why isn't he in here?"

"Honestly, ma'am, I don't know," he said truthfully.

"Ok. Joseph, as it stands, you're my point man on this."

"Really?" Joseph blurted before he could compose himself.

Gilham permitted herself a small smile. She liked Joseph. Potential there.

"Yes Constable. You. I want you to send Hogan in here and then I want you to find out who knew that the money was in the offices last night. It can't be a long list." She turned to face the window that looked out over a small neatly kept garden where photos could be taken when nice press releases were required. "You still here Joseph?" She said without facing him.

"N… No, Ma'am. I'm on it."

Joseph saluted the back of his Chief and walked out. Wow. How did that happen? At least Hogan was gonna get it in the neck now. Prick.

Smudger finished his burger and slurped down the last of his caffeine-laden soft drink. "Ahhhh," he exhaled, "That's better!" Kammy munched away the other side of the small melamine table. He was too invested in stuffing his face to properly acknowledge his companion.

Smudger picked up his phone and dialled the number labelled 'Volvo.' After two rings the other end picked up.

"Hello?" The man on the other end said.

"Ah, is that Mr Ratcliffe?"

"Speaking," said the soft polite voice.

"Hello there. I emailed you last week about coming to see your P eighteen hundred that you have for sale."

"Oh yes. She is still available."

"Perfect. Would you happen to be in this evening?"

"Well, my wife has a pilates class at five and I need to pick up some cat food…"

"Say six pm?" Smudger prompted, bored by the man's waffle.

Ratcliffe sounded uncertain, "It will be dark by then. Are you sure you want to view the car in the dark?"

"It'll be fine, honestly. I don't have much spare time, so I am keen to see it."

"Oh, okay then. If you meet me at the supermarket by the train station, at least there will be car park lighting…"

"Good idea," agreed Smudger.

"Six o'clock then?"

"See you there."

Chapter 9

Quinn parked his car in a small pay and display outside of the main Reading town centre and walked a convoluted path to the shop. Old habits die hard and making sure you were not being followed was one of those habits. He could have parked closer and taken a more direct route which would have saved him 20 minutes, but he had the time. He stopped for a burrito before heading to the tattoo parlour where he had an appointment at 3pm. He arrived at 2.45 and took a seat in the small waiting area at *Stained Ink*. There was an overweight girl who was about 25 years old, he reckoned. She smiled at him and he returned the pleasantry. Time to get into character.

"Hi," he said cheerily. "What are you getting today?"

She was eager to chat it seemed. "Hi there! I'm here for candy!"

Figures, he thought. "I'm sorry, what do you mean?" he asked feigning interest.

She giggled. "I'm having a large candy cane on my arm and the characters from the Animaniacs cartoon are sliding down it like the cane was a slide, ya know?"

He honestly had no fucking idea what an Animaniac was or why you would want any of that on your arm.

"Sounds great!" he said instead.

"What about you? What are you getting?"

"I don't know," he said honestly.

"Really?!?" She said, incredulous, "Is this your first tattoo?"

"How'd you guess?" he smiled as nicely as he could.

She giggled again. "I'm good at reading people."

"Really?" Again, feigning interest. "In that case, what is it that I should get, based on your reading of me?"

"Hmmmm," she said, deep in thought. She studied him carefully, noting the faded scar by his left ear. "I'd say a ying yang thing, although not so mainstream as the classic symbol. You look like you're conflicted over something. Like you're at a junction and you don't know which way to go. The devil is inside most of us... but I sense you fight to try and keep him at bay. A good man though..."

He just stared blankly at her but inside he was vaguely impressed.

"I'm sorry..." she apologised, "I get carried away. I hope I haven't offended you..."

He gave her a reassuring smile. "Not at all. Although I still don't know what tattoo to get. Suggestion?"

She looked genuinely relieved. "Oh ok, of course, Um… how about on your arm a spartan helmet? Except that one side is the skull from the Punisher?"

"The what?"

"You don't know the Punisher? He's a comic book character…?"

"Sorry, no. Would it look cool though?"

"Hell yeah!" she said enthusiastically.

He shrugged. "Sold. That's what I'll ask for."

"Really?! That is so cool. You should look the Punisher up though… "

"I will, although I kinda get the gist from the name."

She laughed sheepishly, "I guess so."

They were interrupted by a heavily tattooed pink-haired woman in her late forties who said, "Okay you two. You're both going in now."

"Great!" his artistic mind reader said. "Good luck!"

He smiled as he got up and followed the girls through to the back where the reclining leather chairs were.

"Please take a seat here," she said to him, pointing to a seat in the corner. "Woody will be with you shortly."

He sat and watched the two girls cross over the room and go behind a screen. Where was she having her crazy tattoo that would necessitate a privacy screen?! Or was that normal practice in a tattoo parlour?

His thoughts were interrupted by a wiry, ginger man who had colourful tattoos right up round his neck. The bright green beanie barely covered the shocks of ginger hair and the overly small black T-Shirt depicting an angel being molested by the devil on it barely covered, well, anything. His jeans were those of the modern 'man', tight and low cut. Utterly ridiculous.

"Hey man!" the tattooist greeted him enthusiastically. "I'm Woody and I'll be inking you today." He offered a wiry and cold hand which he took, careful not to crush it.

Was this really the right guy? He questioned himself.

"What are we doing for you today? Got some ideas?"

Woody sat down on a stool and faced him. He seemed eager to please and eager to talk. Perfect.

"Yeah, actually. The girl who just went behind the screen there suggested a half spartan mask and half Punisher symbol. You know what that is?"

Woody laughed. Then stopped abruptly when he realised he wasn't joking. "Oh. For real? It's a great idea. Will look really cool. You really don't know what the Punisher is, yet you're going to have the symbol tattooed on you?"

"Sure."

"MAN! That is super fucking cool. Ok, you're gonna love it! If you could just sign this and we'll get on it." Woody handed him a form on a clipboard. "It's just insurance stuff. Ya know, so you don't sue me etc."

"Sure," he said again.

"Ok man! I'll go knock up a sketch ready to go. Where are we doing the tat?"

He pointed towards is upper right arm.

"Cool man. Back in a jiffy." With that Woody disappeared back from wherever he had come from, leaving him alone to sign the paperwork and wait for his first ever tattoo. All because he needed information. The tat better look good at least.

Woody could talk. He merrily stencilled the outline of the tattoo onto his arm and had him check it in the mirror to make sure he was happy. So that's the Punisher. He had seen it somewhere before. It actually looked pretty cool.

"Ok," Woody said, his seemingly never waning enthusiasm bordering on annoying. "Ya ready?"

"Go for it."

Wow. That was surprising. It didn't hurt – it was kinda like a cat scratching him.

"You ok, man?" Woody checked, pausing momentarily.

"Yeah, man. No worries. It's not too bad is it?"

"Nah! You get used to it. Sucks in some places mind you… but the arm here isn't one of them."

The buzzing of the tattoo… gun? Needle? Was the only sound for a while before Woody inevitably started talking again. "So, what do you do man?"

Bingo. Here goes.

"Nothing exciting. Just do security pickups. Ya know, from banks and jewellers and the like."

"Oh, cool" Woody enthused. "Is that here in Reading?"

"Yeah, mostly," he nodded, "and the surrounding area. Get a lot of stuff around Windsor. Lot of money around there ya know?"

Woody laughed knowingly, "Yeah, yeah. Tourists, the wealthy bastards and the royals. Shit loads of money."

"Some days I don't know how we get it all in the truck!"

"Really? That much?" Woody was now hanging off his every word. This was too easy!

"Absolutely! You been to Legoland?" He asked, starting to reel the tattooist in.

"Me? Nah. No kids for me mate. Why's that?"

"Ah well you see, it's their special nights at the moment because of bonfire night… "

"Yeah, yeah. They have the fireworks, right?" Now he was leaning forward a touch more. He had him for sure.

"That's right. Mental. It gets so busy that we have to do special runs for them." He paused just briefly and then started on it. "And you know what bugs me? They just expect us to do the fucking overtime! Like I don't have nothing better to do at one in the fucking morning! Maybe I wanna beer ya know? I don't want to do the OT, but they threaten you with reducing your hours…"

"Bastards," was all Woody could say. Oh, he was interested alright.

"Sorry to get all annoyed man. They just take the piss…"

Woody acted like he was just helping him air his woes but started fishing, "So you have to do the pickup at 1am?"

He sighed as if the whole thing got him down. "Yeah. They need time to do the banking after a busy night. Hell, if I had to process half million, it'd take me a lot longer! They do pretty well. I feel sorry for the poor sap who works security at night. Can't just put his feet up… has to wait for us twats to turn up."

Woody shook his head in mock disbelief, yet he could tell the dropping in of the half million grabbed his attention. "Poor bastard…and they just leave the one guy…?"

"Crazy ain't it? Guess they think the security there is tight enough without any extra bods. Cost cutting I guess."

Again, Woody showed mock shock. "Happens all over, the cost cutting that is. The season will be over soon though mate."

"Yeah, but then it's Christmas! Shit gets crazy again!"

The pair descended back into silence. He knew he had planted the seed and that Woody couldn't wait to finish and tell the rest of his crew. Now to just watch and wait. The tattoo was soon finished, and he had to say he was genuinely pleased with it. He thanked Woody, paid and left. He never did see where the chubby girl had her tattoo…

Chapter 10

Charlie Duke had been to most incidents he ever thought he could go to. Fifteen years as a firefighter had served up house fires, boat fires, floodings, road traffic collisions, kids stuck in trees, lock-ins, lock-outs, people stuck in everything from lifts and swings to handcuffs and areas of genitalia in, well, all kinds of stuff! This one though was new.

On the face of it this was just another car fire. It was as routine as it got for the fire service, but this one had a pretty gruesome discovery.

The secluded spot on the fringes of the Royal Great Park indicated to the crew that it was a stolen car taken for a joyride, abandoned and set on fire. There wasn't much left of the once beautiful Volvo p1800; the fire had taken care of the interior, tyres, glass, trim and had reduced the once stunning paintwork to its bare metal.

Duke had been wearing breathing apparatus that night so had been the one to put the fire out and he had also been the one to find the odd way of locking the boot. The boot had been jammed shut with something. It had been driven through the top down into the frame of the car. That 'thing' was a sai.

Duke pressed the talk button on his face mask.

"Boss, receiving," he said into the sealed positive pressure mask.

"Go ahead, Duke," came back his crew manager's disinterested voice through his earpiece.

"Boss, you might want to come look at this," he said, pointing at the boot for all to see.

"On my way over."

His boss walked over from the back of the pump where he had been chatting to the pump operator and sidled up to Charlie.

"What the fuck is that?" he asked, bewildered.

"I think it's a sai, boss," Charlie said, his voice muffled from the mask.

"As in a ninja's weapon?!"

"That's what it looks like."

"Can you remove it?"

"I can try. I'm guessing there's something in the boot that we shouldn't see…" With that he placed both hands on the weapon and gave it a tug. Nothing. He repositioned his hands and gave the slender weapon a jiggle from side to side, making the hole it had punctured in the metal a little bigger. Satisfied, he pulled again. This time the sai came out. He briefly inspected it before handing it over.

The handle looked thinner than he thought it should be. Perhaps there had been a handle that had been burnt away by the fire. The metal was blackened but intact. Next, he got his gloved hands under the lip of the boot and heaved. With a screeching of complaining metal, the boot lifted.

"Shiiiit," both men breathed.

Crew manager Watkins spoke next, "Don't touch another thing. I'll have to chase the police. This is no longer just a stolen burnt out car."

"No problem, boss," Charlie responded, transfixed by the boot's contents.

"Happy the fire is all out?"

"Yeah. Totally out."

"Good, then leave the hose reel where it is and go drop your set. Nobody touches the car, ok?"

"Gotcha," he acknowledged before walking back to the rest of the crew. It was going to be a long night.

Roger Joseph was coming to the end of his official shift. It had just turned 6pm and it was dark outside already. Roger didn't much enjoy the winter with its short days and cold weather. He was more of a cocktail on the beaches of Cuba kind of guy. Whatever the season, he knew that with the responsibility that the chief had given him, he was going to be here late. His husband was just going to have to cook for himself tonight, he mused. He imagined that meant buying a takeaway… some guys just cannot cook. For some reason people assumed that because he was gay, he could cook. Definitely not true!

He had the list of people that knew the money was going to be stored at the council offices. It was a short list which should make it easier for the chief. He was ushered into the chief's office by his secretary who was shrugging her raincoat on in readiness to leave for the day.

"Ah, Joseph. I wondered where you'd got to," Gilham said, sipping a coffee as she stood by her floor to ceiling window behind her desk.

"Sorry, ma'am. Didn't want to get it wrong," Joseph replied, noticeably nervous.

Gilham waved him over and took the piece of paper from Joseph. She looked it over and took another sip of coffee.

"This all of them?" She asked, eyebrows raised.

"Yes, ma'am. That's everyone who knew that the money was going to be kept at the offices overnight."

Gilham snorted. "That's a list of people who officially knew it was being kept there."

Joseph did not know what to say. Had he fucked up?

Gilham noticed the doubt spread across her constable's face. "Don't worry Joseph. Not your fault," she explained. "This is great, but now we need to assign someone to each person and find out who they may have told, or who may have overheard one of these people talking about it."

Joseph looked relieved. "I see. Would you like me to assign these...?"

"Absolutely Constable. You can also contact the ACU. With the names on this list, we have to assume there was a leak or inside job here."

"Yes, ma'am. Anyone in particular?"

"Second thoughts. I'll make that call. You just concentrate on those five names."

"I'm on it, ma'am." With that Joseph hustled out of the office and went looking for the night shift.

His phone buzzed in his pocket, but he was driving so ignored it. He was heading back to the office after his tattoo, the cling film wrap noisy and uncomfortable under his jacket.

His phone buzzed again. Must be important he thought so pulled over in a layby. He pulled the phone out just as it rang off again.

It was Gilham. Great.

He didn't call back, just waited for the third call. Sure enough the phone buzzed, Gilham's name popping up on the screen between the little green phone symbol and the red one. He touched the green.

"Guv," he answered.

"I've got a case for you," she said, keeping it short.

"Ok."

"When can you get here?"

"Ten minutes."

"Good." She hung up.

He sighed as he put his phone away. He would have to play dumb again.

He walked straight into Gilham's office as her secretary had gone home and her door was wide open.

"Guv," he said as way of greeting.

Gilham looked up from her laptop and gave him a friendly yet strained smile. "Take a seat." She gestured towards the seat he had been in that morning.

"Twice in one day," he said, taking the seat, "Doing something right or wrong?"

"Someone's doing something wrong," she growled handing the piece of paper from Joseph over to him.

He took it and looked at the names. "These are?"

She sighed. "These are the names of the people that knew that the county court was to store a hundred thousand pounds last night after the Webb case had been closed."

"And?" he said, trying to sound like he had no idea what she was talking about.

"And the money was stolen last night."

He paused for effect. "Fucking hell. That's a lot of dough. Why was it there in the first place?"

"There had been suspicions that Webb had people on the inside of the company that were due to move the money. We couldn't take that risk so organised another company, but they couldn't get there until the next morning. It was deemed to be safe enough at the county court for one night."

He looked at the list again. "This list can't be comprehensive," he half stated, half asked.

"Comprehensive in an official manner. I've got Constable Joseph assigning people to each one of those names. Either one of those is a leak, or one of them spoke too loudly. Either way, it will have links to us. Fingers will be pointed. I need you to find who it is sharpish."

"That's not really what my role is… "

"I know what your role is. I'm pre-empting your department's involvement. We can both see where this is pointing, so I want you on it now."

"You'll let my guv know?"

"Of course. I'll call Dickson now."

"Very well," he said, standing, "I'll get straight on it."

"Appreciated."

He hadn't even reached his office when his phone buzzed again. "Fuck off!" he cursed, reaching into his pocket. It was Evans.

"Miss me already, Evans?" he said into the phone as he reached his office door.

"Shut up. I don't know why I'm giving you the heads up here, but there's been another sai incident."

That stopped him in his tracks. "Where?"

"Great park. Car fire. Firefighters found it slammed into the boot. They pulled it out and found a body."

"Fuck. Any other notes?"

"Not got there yet. I'll let you know."

"Fuck that. Send me the address." He hung up on Evans.

He slumped into his chair and rubbed his temples. He was supposed to be out watching Woody tonight but now he had this *and* the county court case to look into. Luckily, he already knew where the leak was for that but needed to be seen to be investigating it properly. His phone vibrated on his desk. Evans had been a good little boy and sent the address. He was out the door before the screen had time to go blank again.

"It's me, Zippy," Woody said into his phone.

"Speak," Geoffrey said.

"I've got something," Woody said excitedly.

"10pm. The Griffin pub."

"Ok, I'll be there."

"Don't be late."

"How'd it go, boss?" Kammy asked.

Smudger smiled evilly. "All the money was in the car still and now we have it back."

Kammy nodded enthusiastically. "And the owner?"

"You smell the smoke on me?"

"Yeah…"

"Mr Ratcliff is no longer with us. He's probably at one with his beloved car by now. I love a good fire!"

"He seemed like a ponce anyway. Where to now?"

"The boot is getting full and it's getting late. Find us a place to stay Kammy."

"Right-o, boss." He steered the BMW off the slip road and headed towards Bracknell.

He pulled off the main road and onto a track. The trees in the distance were lit up with the flashing of blue lights. The track was rough and bumpy, and his ageing Rover coupe did not much like it. He eased the motor further down the track and soon he had arrived at the scene. The fire engine must have come in the other way as it was a single-track road and the pump was the other side of the burnt-out car. He pulled up behind Millen's car and got out. He could feel eyes on him from the fire crew and the two detectives who were now speaking to a firefighter. He picked his way around the muddy puddles where the firefighters had used water and stuck his head into the main body of the car before moving on and joining the detectives.

"Millen. Evans." He acknowledged the two coppers.

They barely acknowledged him before saying, "This is Crew Manager Watkins. He was just telling us what happened."

The firefighter glanced at him before speaking, "As I said, this was a routine call on the face of it. Car fire in the woods called in by a jogger. Our control called the jogger back and she reiterated that she did not see anyone or anything other than the car well alight. We arrived, put water on it and then Charlie over there found the sai." He gestured towards a tall well-built firefighter who was leaning against the back of the pump. To his surprise the man was smoking a cigar.

"Can we speak to him?" Evans asked.

"Sure," Watkins said. "Duke, over here will ya?"

The man gracefully pushed away from his leaning pose and walked over, cigar hanging from his mouth.

"Alright fellas?" He greeted them. He had the air of a confident yet laid back man.

"So, you found the sai?" Millen asked

"Yeah. Weird as fuck. We had to loosen the thing before we could pull it out. Once we did, that's when we found the poor bastard."

"Are you saying you've identified the body as a male?" Millen asked, incredulous.

"Have you not looked yet?" Duke asked back.

"No…"

"Well, the body won't give you any clues unless you're a forensic scientist I guess, but me and the boys searched the internet locally for one of these cars. Pretty rare thing. Turns out one is for sale in Windsor. Our money is this is that car. Took it out for a test drive, killed the fella and then set it on fire."

Evans and Millen were stunned into silence. "Impressive," Quinn said. "And the sai?"

Duke turned to face him directly and took a long drag on the cigar. "That's a good question and one for you guys to figure out I guess."

"You don't have a theory?" he probed.

Duke looked back at him as if he were assessing him, weighing him up. He liked this man.

"Like I said, that's your bag, but if I was to hazard a guess, and because this weapon is quite unique, it was a message. A sign. That couldn't have been cheap can it? You wouldn't just slam it in there for the craic, would you? Nah, that's a message I reckon. A pretty good lead I imagine too, no?"

He smiled at the firefighter. Turns out not all fireboys were dumb.

100

Millen interrupted. "And the sai is where now?"

"Wrapped in plastic salvage sheeting," Watkins replied, "On the back of the pump."

"Good. Let's have a look at the body, shall we?" Millen continued.

The five of them circled round to the back of the car. What was left of the wheels dug into the sodden ground and the remains of melted trim made little artistic features on the bare metal frame. All the glass had gone and really all that was left was the metal core of the seats and the engine block. Most of the ancillary equipment had perished in the fire.

"We lowered the boot after we found him. Offered some kind of dignity in death, I guess," Watkins pointed out. "Duke, do you mind?" he asked the still smoking firefighter. Without a word the big man grasped the boot and lifted it.

"Wow," Evans breathed.

The unfortunate man had been baked. The skin and fat had all cooked off leaving the charred pink muscles, tendons and sinew for all to see. The stomach wall had gone too and so the internal organs were starting to slip out of the cavities that they should always be. The scalp and half of the face were missing, leaving behind vacant sockets where eyeballs once were.

"Look at the position of his hands," Millen said, "Looks like they had been tied at the wrist."

"Bastards," Evans cursed, "Do you think he would have suffered?"

Duke took this one. "Depends really. Was he conscious when the fire was lit? If he had been then the smoke may well have knocked him unconscious before heat or flame reached him. Judging by the state of the sai, It looks as though it was slammed in there before the fire took hold, just in case he woke up and tried to escape. Honestly, you hope that was the case, don't you? Imagine how hot it would have been. He would have baked in that box before the flames actually got to the corpse. Because that's all it would have been by that point."

"Have you seen anything like this before?" Quinn asked the firefighter.

Duke shook his head "Baked and fried bodies. Yes. In the boot of a car? No."

"Thanks guys. Evans and Millen will take some details off you…"

Millen and Evans scowled at him as he walked off to circle the scene. He knew it had to be here somewhere. They wouldn't go to the trouble of placing the sai and then not leave a note. A clue. A taunt. His thoughts were interrupted by the firefighter.

"What ya looking for?" Duke asked, lighting another cigar.

He turned to face the firefighter and slipped his own pack of cigars out of his jeans pocket. Duke raised his eyebrows. "Don't come across many cigar smokers," he remarked, offering up his wind proof lighter to the cop.

"Thanks," he said, lighting the slim cigar and taking a drag. "I was thinking the same."

They both stood for a moment in silence. Assessing each other as men. As professionals. There was no love lost between the two services, but there was an unspoken respect between the two men. Unusual but not impossible.

Duke broke the silence. "So, what are you looking for?"

He decided to trust the firefighter. "A note. This isn't the first crime scene involving a sai. In fact it's not the first today. The murderer has been leaving notes behind. Taunting me directly. This scene can't be any different. Obviously, it wouldn't have been in or on the car as it wouldn't have survived, so it must be around here somewhere."

"Not the first today?!" Duke seemed genuinely shocked.

"Sadly not."

"Well, you 'aint gonna see shit out here without some lighting. I'll grab a couple of torches and get the guys to circle the pumps mast light round to wherever we are."

He was suddenly thankful to have this Duke character around. Helpful, confident, clearly not an imbecile and had no idea he was ACU. Even if he did, it probably wouldn't mean anything to him. "That would be great," he thanked the firefighter as he watched him stride back towards their appliance.

While he was gone, he grabbed his phone. Eight o'clock. Shit. He needed to find Woody. He flicked on the tracker app again and selected the latest name in the list. Woody. It zoomed in to Reading and settled on an apartment block in Earley, one of the suburbs of Reading. It was where he lived. Good. He hadn't gone anywhere yet and he doubted the others would gather at his place. He still had time.

"Alright?" Duke asked, handing him a torch.

"Yeah, cheers."

"So, what are we looking for exactly?"

"Well, the previous notes were photos. That's not to say this will be the same, but it'll be similar, I'm sure."

"Well if it is here, it won't be far away will it? Sounds like this dick wants you to find the... clues?"

"Agreed."

The two men ventured two metres into the trees and bushes, sweeping their torches across the ground and up over the trees. The spotlight from the fire appliance followed them as best it could, the trees blocking the powerful beam of light. They had started directly in line with the boot and swept in an anti-clockwise direction towards the driver's door side. Just as they got parallel with the driver's door, Duke's torch picked up something on a tree roughly two metres further into the woodland.

"You see that?" Duke asked his companion.

"I did. Something metallic," Quinn agreed, suddenly interested. They both shone their torches in the direction they had been drawn to. "There!" he exclaimed. They hurried towards their target.

"That'll be it then," Duke remarked as they both looked at the tree. At shoulder height a car key, presumably the Volvo's key, had been stabbed into the soft bark of the Horse chestnut. There was a single metal split ring commonly found on keys and that had been pierced through and looped through a piece of folded paper. He pulled a small knife from his jacket and flicked it open. He slipped the end of the knife through the metal loop and gently pulled the key from the bark.

"Gotcha," he remarked. The two men walked back to where the others were and handed it to Evans who had pulled on a latex glove.

Everyone gathered round now, including the two firefighters who had up until this point remained out of the way and silent. They all watched as Evans carefully removed the paper from the ring and handed the paper to Millen who also had latex gloves on. He in turn carefully opened the folded piece of A4 paper. Out slid a 50 pound note which Millen managed to catch before it hit the ground.

"Good hands," Duke remarked.

Millen held out the unfolded piece of paper so only the cops could see it.

"Ah, come on!" Duke cursed

"Let 'em see it," Quinn told Millen.

"Fine." Millen turned it so that all could see.

"Jesus fucking Christ!" blurted one of the unnamed firefighters.

He had seen the image a million times in his dreams, in his nightmares and every time he closed his eyes. Firefighters saw death and suffering frequently enough, but pure brutality? Probably not.

"Who is it?" The second unnamed firefighter asked, his voice shaky.

Millen and Evans exchanged uncomfortable glances.

He had many things to hide, but this was not one of them. "It's my brother."

"Duuuude," Duke said "I'm so sorry…"

He shrugged "It's been a while now, so don't worry."

"But still…" Duke tailed off.

He gave the firefighter a reassuring smile. 'It's ok' kinda thing.

Watkins spoke up now, "And whoever did this," he gestured towards the burnt-out car, "did that to your brother?!"

He shook his head "No… but yes. He didn't do it himself, but had it done."

"What an absolute cunt," Duke spat. Everyone nodded furiously, uncertain to what they should, or could say. "And now he's taunting you with it?"

"Looks that way."

"Why?"

"Why does anyone taunt anyone? To get a rise." Everyone was silent now.

"What I don't get," Evans broke the silence, "is how this one is a clue…?"

107

"Agreed," Millen added. "The other one was a clear link between the two scenes, where this one doesn't have any bearing, surely?"

They all looked at the photo again. It was a close up of his brother's face. His face was laid on the floor, his cheek squished against the blood-stained wood. His mouth was agape as if he had been caught mid scream. His green eyes stared at the viewer, lifeless and yet pleading for help at the same time. The whites of his eyes were stained with the pooling blood that ran from his auburn hair. His hair that was matted with the blood from the gaping hole where his temple should have been.

Duke asked, "What, if you don't mind me asking, caused the injury?"

"That was done with a lucky eight ball from my brothers pool table. Ironic, huh?" he replied, trying to add a lightness to the situation. He had, after all, been dealing with this for years. These guys were fresh to the horror.

"Then I think we have our link," Watkins murmured.

"Sorry?" Evans asked, half because he didn't hear and half because he wanted the man to go on.

Watkins Expanded. "Did you notice what was left of the gear knob on the car?" he asked.

"Not really…" Evans admitted.

"To me," Watkins said with some trepidation in his voice, "That gear knob was one of those aftermarket cue ball ones."

The man exchanged glances. Watkins turned to Duke for support "Duke? That's what you reckon too, yeah?"

"I have little doubt about it," the burly firefighter agreed.

Evans and Millen went over to look in the car.

"Do you have the link to the car sale advert you mentioned?" He asked the fire crew.

"Sure!" One of the unnamed men said, pulling his phone out of his leggings pocket. He proceeded to search his phone. "Here!" he said, handing his phone over to him.

Sure enough, there was an advert for a Volvo P1800. He scrolled through the pictures until he came to one of the interior. Clear as day the auto gearbox selector was not a ball. It was your standard gear lever knob shaped like an Ice cream cone.

Millen called out, "Looks like a ball to me."

Quinn hustled over to the car where his colleagues stood. Millen pointed at what remained of the gear selector, "Ball," Millen said flatly.

"You have any gloves?" he asked the two detectives. Holding his hand out while he looked inside of the car through what was left of the driver's window. He felt the presence of someone next to him. It was Duke.

"What are ya thinking?" Duke asked.

"Honestly?" he replied, snapping the latex gloves on, "I have no idea, but seeing as the gear knob has been swapped, there must be *something.*"

He reached in and grasped the remains of the gear knob. He figured it was a screw-on one and gave it an experimental twist anticlockwise. He felt a slight movement, so he braced and twisted. Miraculously the ball turned.

Duke shook his head in disbelief. "How is that not melted on?"

"No idea, but I'll take a win when I can." Thirty seconds later and the ball came off and he pulled himself back out from the window. Millen and Evans had gathered round, joining Duke in looking at the ball. Nobody spoke. He slowly turned the charred and partly melted ball over in his hands. It was just a ball with a thread for screwing onto the stick.

"Anything?" Millen asked.

"Don't see anything myself," Evans quipped. He almost sounded happy that there wasn't a clue there.

Duke spoke up again, "I don't get it."

Then Watkins made everyone turn around. "What if…"

"Go on…" Millen urged

"Well, what if it's not the cue ball we want. What if it was the original gear-knob we want…?"

Everyone looked around at each other, annoyed that they hadn't thought of that themselves.

Lobbing the cue ball at the unsuspecting Evans, he walked over and slapped Watkins on the back. "Brilliant. Great spot."

The young officer almost blushed, "Thanks… but where is it?"

Chapter 11

The cheap hotel in Bracknell was simple but clean and Kammy immediately flicked the kettle on while Smudger hooked up the Wi-Fi.

"Coffee, boss?" Kammy asked as he emptied a sachet into a plain white mug.

"Yeah," Smudger replied sitting down on one of the beds, his phone in his hand.

"Where are we gonna stash the money?"

"Lloyd's," Smudger replied without looking up from his phone.

"In a bank?!" Kammy asked bewildered.

"Don't be stupid," Smudger snorted, "Owusu's."

"Ah, that makes more sense…"

Smudger didn't look up. Christ, Kammy was dumb sometimes. Loyal though. Right now he would take that. "You'll take the money over to him while I find our next target." Kammy looked dismayed.

"Don't I get to come along? I'll miss all the fun!"

Smudger now looked up. "I'll need you for the next job. You won't miss out."

"Oh good… " Kammy answered slightly embarrassed. Then added, "What is the next motor?"

"The ZX."

"Oh man. I loved that car."

"Me too… I've just got to find it…"

Kammy left a moment of silence before handing over a cup of coffee and asking. "And the other thing?"

"His time is coming soon… I'm gonna rip his fucking throat out."

Roger Joseph sat at his desk wondering when he would be able to go home. He was now well into overtime but relished the opportunity to prove his worth.

He had dished out the leads to detectives. On his list he had Victoria Sinton who was the District Judge who preceded over the Webb case. She was assigned to Detective Lee Harvey. Next there was Eddie Hutchinson who was the CEO of *Sterling Securities* who were the new company that were to pick up the 100 grand. He was assigned to Detective Kayleigh Osbourne. Third was Harlee Dean, the caretaker and sometime light security for the County Court. He was assigned to Detective Nico

Yennaris. Fourth was Barry Ashby, the prosecuting lawyer for *Webb and Webb* whose money it was originally. Ashby had been assigned to detective Pat Kruse. That left one more name, other than Gilham herself. That person was Ruth Stanislaus, Gilham's secretary.

Joseph felt bad about Ruth being on the list, but figured it wasn't the first time as, being Gilham's secretary, she was privy to a great many things. She was probably used to it! Anyway, he had assigned Kevin Godfrey to her. He was a detective who was close to retirement and was known for being a big softy. Joseph hoped that he would go easy on Ruth.

What he didn't know how to go about was what to do with Gilham? Was he supposed to assign her a Detective? Could he authorise an investigation into the chief inspector? He certainly did not want to, and her name was not on the list he had given her… He decided to ask the night Sergeant – thankfully Manual had gone home. He lifted the receiver on his desk and called extension 410. After three rings the desk sergeant picked up. "Mahon" a deep and soulful voice answered

"Mahon, it's Joseph. How are you?"

"Ah, Joseph. What are you still doing here?"

"OT while I help out the chief… " he was cut off mid-sentence by Mahon.

"Oooo, rockin with the big cheese are ya?"

Joseph chuckled, "In a manner of speaking." Joseph outlined his task to Mahon and finished by asking if he should assign a detective to Gilham.

"I wouldn't," Mahon sighed. "Gilham will have already contacted ACU and informed them of the situation. What case is this?"

"I can't really say… " Joseph said sounding apologetic.

"Good lad," Mahon said approvingly. "Anyway, like I said, she would have contacted the ACU so it's out of your hands… anyway, shouldn't Hogan have dealt with this?"

"You'd of thought so, wouldn't you?" Agreed Joseph. "Anyway, thanks Gav, appreciate the help. Have a good night, mate."

"Anytime," Mahon said before hanging up.

Good, thought Joseph. He had not wanted to deal with that situation! The Anti-Corruption Unit were welcome to the case although he knew they wouldn't find anything. Everyone respected the Chief. He pinged off an email to Gilham detailing who he had assigned to who and packed up his gear. Home at last.

Quinn had left Evans and Millen to figure out where the original gearstick was. It was approaching 9pm now and he needed to go find Woody. His tracker had shown that the tattooist had left his flat and was on the move.

The rush hour traffic had subsided, so he made good time heading back into Reading. It looked as though Woody was on a bus. The tracker stopped every half a mile or so and it was heading towards the town centre.

He gambled that the centre was his destination, so parked up in the same spot he had used when visiting Woody earlier in the day. He walked past the burrito bar he had visited earlier, his stomach grumbling, but he cast that feeling to the back of his mind while he mulled over the gearstick question.

Where could it be? What did it have to do with anything? Maybe there wasn't anything else to it. Maybe whoever it was just swapped the stick for the eight ball at his brother's deathbed. Seemed like a lot to go through seeing as they had already found the photo. He felt like it wasn't just taunting though. He was convinced that the murderer wanted him to follow clues, to play a game with him.

His thoughts were disturbed by a beep from his phone. The tracker had been still for over two minutes now and was warning him of the fact. He zoomed in on the map. He had stopped at The Griffin pub. He didn't know it especially well. Head down, he headed for the pub.

He sat on a stool at the far end of the old wooden bar nursing a pint of stout. The pub was quite busy, with probably 30 people in total chatting and drinking. The bar had been done out with subtle movie nostalgia. From the odd film poster of straight to DVD movies and a cocktail list that featured drinks such as 'The Top Gun' and 'The Shawshank'. It was in need of refurbishment, but still clung on without looking run down.

There were six booths along the main wall opposite the bar. Between them were twelve tables of various sizes in the four metres between bar and booths. Woody sat alone in the fifth booth from the stained-glass front door. That left one booth to the right of Woody's that had three women sat clinking glasses full of white wine. Woody had a pint of lager of some sorts that he had barely touched. His focus seemed to be on his phone that he stared at intently.

He glanced around the pub and made sure there wasn't anyone that he knew in there. It was only Woody that would recognise him. That made things simpler. He himself had a baseball cap pulled down tightly that cast his face into shadow, and he kept his body hunched over his pint of black stuff while he feigned interest in the cocktail menu.

His eyes flicked toward the stained-glass door as it opened. In stepped the one known as Matthew. Of course, that wasn't his real name. His real name was Martin Rowland a PPO within Thames Valley Police. A

PPO was a Principle Protection Officer within the firearms unit. A PPO headed up a team made up of AFO's or Authorised Firearms Officers. George and Bungle were AFO's. Technically Rowland was a CTSFO – Counter Terrorist Specialist Firearms Officer but, seeing as he headed up a unit he was known as the PPO. Wasn't exactly a catchy term was it? He thought, smirking into his drink as he took a rare slurp.

Rowland spotted Woody and nodded in his direction before moving to the bar to order his own drink. He had come alone.

Rowland sat down opposite Woody and they began to talk. They didn't bother to converse in hushed tones as there was enough background noise in the bar to mask their conversation. Shit. He needed to get closer. He signalled the barman and asked for a bottle of champagne and three glasses. He took them and paid in cash before quickly rising out of his seat and heading to the booth with the three women sat in it, bottle and glasses clutched in his hands. He kept his head low so that Rowland would not recognise him and ducked down into the booth where three startled women were about to complain. He had to act quickly so as not to draw attention to himself.

"Hello ladies," he said in way of greeting, and hurriedly continued before they could reply. "My friend at the bar there wanted to buy you three a drink but is too embarrassed to come over himself. Shy fella ya know? His wife recently divorced him after shagging his brother and so his confidence is low. Anyway," he continued barely drawing breath while trying to lend one ear to the booth next to them. "He sent me over. I'm Andy." He put the three glasses and the champagne down on the table and smiled as warmly as he could. Rowland had briefly looked up but almost immediately looked back at Woody. If he had recognised him then he masked it well.

"Which one is your friend?" Asked the woman to his right. He looked at her more closely now. She was pretty, perhaps 28 years old with dark curly hair. She wore small rectangular glasses that sat high up her slender nose. Her dark eyes looked playful and the lightly shimmered lips looked lush. He smiled at her and turned towards the bar. He picked up snippets from the booth next door 'Legoland' and 'tattoo' being two of them.

He pointed along the bar to a young man who was laughing at something the man to his left has said. "That's him" he said, his finger picking out the man wearing a bright blue shirt with some kind of detail on it. The shirt was tucked into dark denim jeans that became ridiculously narrow at the ankle which made his moccasin boots look huge. The back of his head had been shaved tightly, rising into a thick wad of tousled blonde hair. His side profile revealed a clean-shaven face that looked happy and free of worry.

"Not bad," one of the other women quipped, pouring the champagne into the three glasses.

"Who's he interested in?" said the third as she accepted a glass from her friend.

"Or is this some kind of blanket flirting? Fishing, hoping to catch anything?" asked the spectacled woman.

He laughed, hoping his eyes looked warm and friendly. 'When?' he overheard. That sounded like Rowland. He was desperately straining his ears now. "He wouldn't say" he said to the women. "He's not one to cast a net though. It will be one of you specifically."

The champagne pourer was speaking but he didn't hear what she said. He was focusing everything he had on trying to hear what was being said in the adjoining booth. Woody spoke. "Thursday night."

Gotcha.

He was suddenly back in the room, feeling all three women staring at him "Well?" The Spectacled one asked.

"Sorry, what?" he asked apologetically. "My apologies, I thought I heard, um, a familiar voice… " He watched as Rowland downed his pint, stood up and walked out of the pub. He didn't give him a second look. Good.

"What is his name?" The Spectacled woman asked presumably for the second time

"Oh, sorry, it's Stuart. Stuart Nelson," he lied. He had no idea who the fella was or what his name was.

Woody stood up and headed to the Stained-glass doors.

"Anyway," he added. "My work here is done. Good luck ladies." With that he smiled and nodded at the three women and took his leave. As he walked past the man in the skinny jeans he leant in and spoke in his ear. "You see that table of three women? The one in the glasses thinks you're hot. Good luck." With that he walked out of the pub without looking back.

He saw Woody stride off towards the town centre. He was tempted to tail him but thought better of it. He had what he needed. With that he dug his hands into his pockets and headed back off to his car.

Chapter 12

Kammy was heading back to the hotel after dropping off the money to Owusu. Owusu was a friend of the old gang who Smudger trusted implicitly. Kammy himself never really liked Owusu, but then again, he didn't really like anyone. He feared Smudger as much as liking him, but the boss had always looked after him so he couldn't complain. Hell, he'd taken a shank to the ribs for the boss, so he reckoned he was owed anyway.

The way he saw it, once they had collected all the money, he'd be off to an island somewhere. Cape Verde had always intrigued him. Maybe there, or perhaps the Caribbean. That would be fucking amazing.

What he was keen to avoid was this running feud with the cop. Kammy just could not understand the risk the boss was taking. He had exacted revenge by having his family brutally murdered. Why did he feel the need to go after the man himself? To what end? Kammy presumed Smudger wanted to kill him himself. He supposed he got that, but why leave all these clues as to what they were doing?

The last one, the gear knob from that old shit car, was one step too far for Kammy's liking. Why bother? Why not just track the cop and kill him? Why did he need to taunt the man before giving him a chance to fight? Surely it would be easier to grab all the money, shoot the bastard and run off into the night to enjoy the wealth? He really did not get it.

Whatever the motives, he had dutifully left the parcel at the pick-up point as he had been asked. His train of thought and the heavy metal music he was blaring through the Beamer's speakers was interrupted by the phone ringing. It was the boss.

"Hello?" He said a bit too loudly as the phone connected.

"Fucking hell, Kammy! No need to shout. Where are you?"

"Ten minutes out from you."

"Good. Well, I've located the ZX. We go tonight so come pick me up."

"Okay, boss." He hung up. "Tonight," he said aloud as the heavy growling of the lead singer came back up to full volume. He wondered where it could be and if he would get a chance to fuck someone up. He smiled evilly. He had tasted blood after the girl at the garage. He wanted more.

He drove the Rover back to the station and made his way to his office. The station was quiet now. He glanced at his watch. 11pm. He pushed his office door open and circled round to his desk. He slumped down into the chair and closed his eyes. Blindly fumbling in his jeans pocket, he pulled out the paper with the list of people that were in the know about the money being stashed. Opening his eyes he looked at the paper and read down the list. He noticed Gilham wasn't on the list but figured that as she had told him about the case, he was already meant to look at her too.

He powered up his computer and clicked on the email tab. There were all kinds of crap that he did not care about. He found the two he wanted.

One was from his boss, Shay Logan, that confirmed that he was on the case. The second was from Roger Joseph detailing who had been assigned who on the list. He scanned down the list and found the name he wanted.

Godfrey.

It immediately looked as though Joseph was looking out for Ruth. Mistake. Godfrey was competent but coming to the end of his career so would need a little nudge. But when to give him that nudge? He needed to get what he was owed first.

Owed? Was that the right word? He didn't linger on that thought, instead, fishing his phone out of his pocket and dialling a number that he memorised. He put the phone to his ear and waited.

"Hello?" the female voice answered.

"It's me," he said, deadpan.

"Oh, hi. Nothing has changed here."

"Good," he said unable to hide the frustration. "Do you need anything?"

"Not yet," the female voice replied, "but soon the Benzodiazepine will run out."

"Noted. The money will be with you soon."

The female voice stayed silent.

"What is it?" he asked, knowing what the answer would be.

Another pause. "Where is it coming from?"

"You know I can't tell you that…"

"Like you always say. I want to reiterate that I don't agree with what you're doing."

"What *am* I doing?"

"Well… never mind. Just make sure nobody… gets hurt, ok?"

"I'll do my best," he said trying to remain calm. This was none of her business. She was paid well for her services *and* her silence.

"Very well. We will see you soon?"

"As soon as I've cleared all my work."

"Very well," she said again. With that she hung up.

He placed the phone on the table and sighed. One day he hoped that the phone call would be more positive. Until that day he just had to keep on doing what he was doing. Keep busy. Keep the money coming in.

His mind turned to his next job. Thursday night. It was Tuesday evening already, so Rowland had very little time to plan his job. That left him with little time too.

How would Rowland do it? Just knock over the Security van? Would they unload the cash into their own vehicle? Would they do it at Legoland or would they wait until it was on the move again?

He figured that the best time would be during the transfer of the money into the truck. Getting into one of those bastards once the driver was back in the cab was nigh on impossible. It had to be at the park. So, driving one of those trucks away would seem like a good idea, but then you'd have to get rid of it, so he was going to have to bank on them bringing their own mode of transport that could move that sort of money. That would mean that he in turn didn't need to bring a van or similar. One less thing to think about. He would need to set up a camera somewhere. He also needed to make sure that the security guard would not get hurt.

A plan started to form in his head. It had its risks, but when hadn't he faced off against the odds? He had to make it work though. One stone, two birds. Or should he say one bird and three fucktards? He smiled to himself. He would enjoy this one.

Smudger climbed into the Beamer as the digital clock on the dash ticked over to 00:36. "Head for Wokingham," he said to Kammy as a way of greeting as he forcefully shut the passenger door.

"Boss," Kammy replied simply slotting the gear knob into drive.

"I assume the parcel was dropped off?"

"Yes, boss," Kammy said keeping it simple.

"Good." He had in his hands a sai. He turned it over slowly, admiring its simplicity and therein its beauty. He tapped the handle before placing it on the floor between his booted feet. "Let's go get some money," he said gleefully.

Kammy turned his head slightly to look at Smudger, pleased to see he was focused on the money for a change. He didn't ask where exactly they were going. The boss would tell him in good time.

Smudger directed Kammy through the town that was now quiet save for the odd car heading who knew where. It was 1am now and the night had settled in. Kammy wondered where the hell they were going. Still he did not speak up. Out the other side of the town they went, keeping the old car to the speed limit so as not to attract any unwanted attention.

"Turn here," Smudger said pointing to the right.

Kammy indicated and looked at the blue, white and red sign that pointed down the road he had been instructed to follow. "They never scrapped it?!" he exclaimed.

"Course not," Smudger admonished. "If they had, we wouldn't be here. The money would be long gone."

"Then why are we here?" Kammy asked, confused. He dutifully pulled into the road and drove down to some large steel gates that blocked the entrance to the scrap yard.

"Because my mentally challenged friend," Smudger began, "the owner collects classic cars. It would appear that he currently owns our ZX."

Kammy switched off the engine and sat staring into the yard. All was quiet. "Do you know where it is exactly?" he asked, not taking his eyes off the immediate surroundings, scanning for movement.

"No, not exactly, but it has to be here somewhere. If he has a collection, then I'm guessing all the cars are in a warehouse."

"Or he's that minted he has enough space at his own pad to keep them," Kammy said without thinking.

"That is true," Smudger mused, "but seeing as his house is that one right there," he said pointing at the mini mansion a hundred metres from the entrance, "Then It's safe to assume the cars are here somewhere."

Kammy looked over at the house. It was large and grandiose. It wasn't pretty though. Money had been lavished upon it but done with no style. It was if a child had been allowed to stick the family diamonds onto a dough house they'd made for a school project.

"Let's go see, shall we?" Smudger said picking up his sai and climbing out of the motor.

"Aye, boss," Kammy replied sheepishly.

They stood at the gates. There was a large padlock looped through the chunky slide lock. They looked around. There was clearly an alarm system of some kind wired into the gates somehow.

"Probably cameras too," Kammy commented.

"I have no doubt of that," Smudger agreed pulling his hood up over his head. "Keep your head down and climb."

The gates were sturdy and climbing them was remarkably easy. They dropped down on the other side and paused for a moment. They didn't sense any movement so continued forward.

To their right was a drive on scale for weighing scrap and beyond that was the main offices and reception for the site. They could make out several small warehouse-looking buildings straight ahead. One was labelled 'Tyres' and another 'Exhausts'. Beyond those buildings to the left they could just see the huge crushers that compacted cars into small cubes. On the right, the site opened-up and they could see the traditional scrap yard setup. Cars were piled three, maybe four vehicles high. Suddenly a bright light came on, lighting up the yard that they now stood, stock still.

"Must be on a sensor," Smudger whispered. They tentatively moved on, noticing signs such as 'Non-ferrous' and 'Batteries'. The stacked cars were in hugely varying states of repair. Some had been stripped to their bare bones while others looked as if you could drive them away.

"Brings back memories of my youth," Kammy whispered.

Smudger nodded his agreement before adding, "See that building over there?" he was pointing at a half-brick and half-corrugated metal structure. They stood just beyond the offices and twenty metres from the unit with 'Tyres' written on it. The building in question was well over to the left of them, half obscured by an old fire engine and a stripped-out helicopter.

"Looks new," Kammy said, staring at the building, "And I bet it has security."

"It has to be that one," Smudger said in agreement. They carefully walked towards the structure. It was maybe fifteen metres wide and two stories high. They couldn't see how far back it went but Smudger figured that it must go some way if he had a car collection in there. Walking around the fire engine they could see that the building had cameras mounted on each corner and the main doors that were on rollers enabling the front to open wide were locked, bolted and chained. This was definitely it.

"There must be a different way of getting in," Smudger said aloud.

"I'll go look round the side here," Kammy indicated, pointing down the right-hand side of the structure.

Smudger nodded his acknowledgement and went left. Neither men found another door or window down the sides and met at the rear to find one small door. This door was opposite a fence that backed onto the mansion Smudger had pointed out when they arrived. In the fence was a gate.

"This must be his private entrance, from house to garage. Fuck this guy has some money," Smudger explained.

"We'll have more," Kammy snorted.

They examined the door and found that it was unsurprisingly locked. This one had a numeric pad that meant it was electronically locked. It would save the rich bastard from needing a key.

"Now what?" Kammy asked, his shoulders sagging.

"We smash the door in and wait for the cavalry," Smudger said simply.

Kammy visibly blanched. Smudger smiled.

"You want the pigs here?" Kammy asked, incredulous.

"Fuck no, obviously. This guy is one of us. He won't want the Police either. He'll deal with it internally. You honestly think all of this is legit?"

"Well, no," Kammy said clearly unsure if his boss was reading this correctly.

"Trust me," Smudger soothed, "We break in, either he or some goons will arrive. We fuck 'em up or make them help. Sometimes we gotta work for our money." Smudger smiled and pulled the sai from his waistband. He swung and slammed the sai into the keypad. It sparked wildly and the face collapsed in on itself, but the door remained shut. "Go grab something to smash this door in," he instructed.

Kammy returned with some unidentifiable car part. It was heavy enough to do the job and moments later they were stood inside.

"No alarm," Kammy said both surprised and relieved.

Smudger snorted derision "It'll be silent you mug. Someone will be with us soon."

The storage unit was impressive. It was clean and cool. The smooth concrete floor had been painted a light battleship grey and the brick walls had been plaster boarded so the dust from the bricks didn't infect the precious motors. Strip lights hung from the high vaulted ceiling yet offered no light. Before them was car after car displayed like a small museum.

"Fuuucking hell," breathed Smudger, "Mk1 transit… and a MK2… they're pristine!"

"Check out the Chevy pickups over there," Kammy cooed, pointing to the right where there were five American V8 pickups, all in perfectly polished condition.

"Christ, there must be a few quid in here…"

"Fuck my life. Look at that!" Smudger was striding towards a beautiful silver super car. Its elegant sweeping lines from its low bonnet to the rear engine bay were a throwback to classic Le Mans cars. "I've never seen one in the flesh." Smudger was close to drooling.

"What is it?" Kammy asked, bewildered.

"WHAT IS IT?" Smudger answered, incredulous without turning his attention away from the gleaming car. "It's a Jaguar XJ220. They were built between 1992 and 1994.

This baby has 3.5 litre twin turbo'ed V6 pushing as standard nearly 550bhp. It was in its day a supercar killer as was it the fastest production car in the world for a brief period of time. Underrated and underappreciated, this is my favourite supercar of all time. I mean, *Look at it!"*

"Yeah… it's not bad," Kammy agreed, walking over to where his boss was gently rubbing his hand along the sloping lines of the car. "I mean, it's no Testarossa or Diablo… "

Smudger didn't seem to hear him; too enamoured by the piece of automotive history in front of him. Neither did he hear three men enter the warehouse. It was only when Kammy tapped him on the shoulder did he seem to come back into the room. "Huh?" He blurted, turning, "Ooohhh," he followed up facing the three men. They were large. Very large. They stood in a line, arms folded over their huge chests, arms the size of elephant trunks. None of them spoke. They just stared at the intruders, blocking the exit.

"Alright fellas?" Smudger began cheerily. "I was just admiring this 'ere Jag. Beautiful car…"

He was cut off by the sound of a thick Irish accent coming from behind the three goons.

"Watchya think ya doin in ma place?" The voice said.

Neither Kammy nor Smudger replied, waiting for the voice to present a face.

"Ah said, what the FUCK are ya doin in ma place?!" The voice said, anger spilling over like a cascading waterfall. Then he came into sight, emerging from behind goon one on the left. The man was dressed in a dressing gown made of green silk; the matching slippers gently putter-patting on the clean grey floor. He was smaller than the goons but was roughly the size of Smudger. The main difference being that the Irishman was bald, and a gut was forming around his waist.

Smudger raised his hands in mock surrender and said, "I was just explaining to the three lads there that I was admiring the Jag... quite a motor isn't it? Does it belong to you Mr O'Conner?"

The dressing gowned man stayed silent, sizing up the two idiots who had broken into his property.

Smudger continued unabated, "In fact, you have quite the collection here. I wonder if you have one car in particular..."

O'Conner was incensed. "If you know who I am, you know what I am capable of... "

Smudger interrupted the Irishman, seemingly unimpressed with the upcoming threat. "It's just that I've been retracing cars that I used to own and collecting what is mine. You see, I believe you have one of my cars."

O'Conner seemed interested now, his anger subsiding. "A car you used ta own ya say? Left something in the glovebox did ya?" He smirked at his humour.

He knows. "Aye, summit like that," Smudger nodded.

"Would it be the Nissan 300 ZX that you seek?"

Shit. "That's the one…"

"Well, ya shoulda said!" O'Conner said enthusiastically. "It's right over there." He pointed to an ancient recovery truck. "Behind the Bedford."

Kammy and Smudger both looked in the direction of the truck, craning their necks in an attempt to see past it.

"Go right ahead," O'Conner encouraged.

Smudger led the way, Kammy nervously in tow.

There it was. The deep purple Nissan 300 ZX. Still a beautiful car. But not intact. At all. Every single part of it had been stripped down. It was all there, just not attached to the car anymore.

Smudger turned, but it was too late. One of the goons smashed Kammy over the back of the head, knocking him clean out.

The second goon was lunging for Smudger. He fainted to his left just in time, the big man crashing harmlessly into the floor. Smudger quickly swivelled and aimed a vicious kick to the man's head, sending his ugly mug cracking backwards. He was lucky it didn't break his neck. He wasn't going to get back up anytime soon..

The man who had taken Kammy out had now raised his fists, challenging Smudger to have a go. Smudger smiled dutifully and raised his own fists.

The big man came at him, swinging a huge right hook. Smudger easily ducked inside the big slow blow and, as the weight of the big man came round onto his leading foot, again Smudger aimed a kick, but this time at the man's knee. The big man buckled, screaming in agony. His defence faltered, his hands grasping for his damaged knee. Smudger didn't waste the opportunity and brought his own right hook crashing down into the man's temple. He joined his colleague on the floor, a crumpled mess.

Smudger set himself again, waiting for the third attack. O'Conner and the last of his guard came round the back of the Bedford. "Done time 'ave ya?" O'Conner asked, "You fight like you have. No mercy. No wasted energy. Impressive. No matter, Colgan here will fuck ya up."

As if that was an order, Colgan came at him. He picked up a tyre iron and swung it wildly at Smudger who had caught the glimpse of metal and had retrieved the sai from his belt, bringing it up to defend himself. The tyre iron came down hard but Smudger caught the rough metal in the scoop between the main shaft and the right prong with clang.

The bigger man's greater strength started to show as he pushed down on Smudger, forcing him to brace with his left leg behind him. He knew he couldn't hold the big man so with a subtle twist of the sai he flicked the tyre iron from Colgan's grasp, knocking Colgan off balance at the same time, his great weight sending him falling into where Smudger had been.

As the man stumbled forward, Smudger dropped to one knee and thrust the sai sideways into Colgan's trailing leg, the ancient Chinese weapon digging deep into the huge thigh.

The man screamed in agony as he hit the floor. The sai had come out as quickly as it had gone in. Smudger swivelled as Colgan hit the floor, striding forward at his stricken foe and brought his leather boot crashing down into his face. Colgan lay prone, out of it. Smudger knelt down and looked at O'Connor. Without hesitation, Smudger brought the sai down in powerful arc and buried the weapon deep into Colgan's right eye. Blood and bodily fluids burst out of the new hole.

Smudger wiped Colgan's blood from the sai on the thug's jeans before looking up at O'Conner. To his credit the Irishman didn't run. Didn't show any fear either. He just stared at Smudger with hate. "Yer a deed man!" He hissed instead.

"Heard it all before," Smudger smiled, slapping Kammy round the face. "Wake up ya dumb fuck," he said with a hint of sentiment. After a second, harder slap, Kammy

138

began to come around at which point Smudger focused his attention on O'Conner. "Now, how about you tell me where my money is?"

Now O'Conner started to back away.

Chapter 13

Smudger had O'Conner pinned up against a beautiful Mk1 Ford Transit, the tip of the gleaming sai pressed against O'Conner's throat, just making the slightest impression on the skin of the Irishman.

"Where is it?" Smudger asked casually

"You come into my home. You beat up my men. You *threaten* ME! ME?!" O'Conner was apoplectic with rage. Snarling at the sheer nerve of the men. "I'm givin you one last chance ta get the fuck off of ma property…"

Smudger wasn't interested. He pushed the sai slightly harder against the prick's throat. "I'm giving *you* one last warning. *Where is my money?!*"

O'Conner spat in Smudgers face.

Quick as a flash Smudger brought his knee violently up into the Irishman's balls, hard and fast. He couldn't crumple. There was a sai pressed against his throat. He groaned in agony. "Ya prick…"

Spittle running down his cheek, Smudger screwed up his face into one of pure anger. "This is your last chance Paddy. Give me what I want, or I'll march over to your pretentious shit hole and find your wife…"

O'Conner steadied himself. "You leave her out of this," he managed through clenched teeth. "I'll give ya what ya want"

"There. That wasn't so hard was it?" Smudger cooed.

"Inspection pit. Far corner. Under the boards. It's all there."

Smudger drew the sai back and grabbed O'Connor by the scruff of the dressing gown and shoved him in the direction he had pointed. Kammy too was up and about now and joined them as they made their way over to the corner. Stacked along one wall were rows of mechanics drawers. The good ones. All red and shiny and filled with all the tools a mechanic could want. These alone would be worth thousands. In front of these lay the boards that covered the inspection pit.

Without being asked O'Conner spoke. "We don't use this for inspecting cars. Nobody does anymore. It just looks the part... and comes in handy for storing stuff."

"Kammy. Get those boards up will ya?" Smudger asked, gesturing with the sai to the boards on the ground.

Kammy 'Harrumphed' and got on with the task. He heaved at each solid wood board that looked like a small railway sleeper and slowly revealed the pit as the other two men looked on. With five boards up they could all see inside the pit, but it was dark.

"Light switch is over there," O'Conner sighed nodding at the wall above the tool racks.

Kammy dutifully went and switched it on. A light flickered on in the pit and Smudger peered in. There, to his delight, was a pile of rucksacks. Maybe 15 bags in total. "Wonderful," Smudger breathed.

"It's all there," O'Conner repeated. "Now get it and fuck off."

"After you," Smudger laughed, pushing O'Conner into the pit. He landed on the bags, cushioning his fall.

"Ya bastard!!" O'Conner screamed. "Am gonna fooking kill ya!"

"Good luck with that," Smudger smirked, "Now be a good paddy and chuck the bags up."

O'Conner fixed him with a stare full of hatred. He knew when he was beat though and began launching the bags out of the pit.

Between the three of them they carried the bags out to the main gate where they forced O'Conner to open it. They loaded the bags into the Beamer and then marched O'Conner back into the yard.

"Over there," Smudger said pushing the Irishman towards the tyre shed. The three of them marched over to the small building. "Saw this in a movie once. Always wanted to try it."

O'Conner looked at him quizzically before realising what they had planned.

"Fa fook's sake… "

Kammy and Smudger slipped car tyres over the head of the man until only his eyes showed. He was stacked up in the middle of the tyres like a hotdog in a bun.

"'Appy now?" O'Conner asked, seething.

"Almost," Smudger said grinning. He sat down on a pile of tyres and turned to Kammy. "Why don't you go get his missus?"

Kammy smiled evilly. Now was his turn to have some fun!

"NO!!" Screamed O'Conner. "Please. Leave her alone. I'll do anything… "

Kammy strode off towards the mansion, rubbing his hands together with glee.

The two men sat in silence, one grinning and the other foaming at the mouth. It was gone midnight by this point but Smudger did not have a care in the world. The only thing on his mind was the thought of sweet revenge. Oh how he was going to enjoy killing that cop. He had spent the best years of his life behind bars because of that man. He had made sure that the cop would suffer as he was for the twenty years he was away for, but now the time had come to punish him once and for all. He had planned and fantasied about it and now it was so close. In one swoop he would claim the last of his money and finally kill the man who had dominated his dreams for so long. But right now he had to lay the last clue. The last little crumb that would lead the filth to his end.

After fifteen minutes Kammy returned to the tyre shed with a blonde woman who was giving him merry hell. Smudger smiled. Feisty one!

O'Connor's face dropped when he saw her. "Lindsay. Did he hurt you?"

She noticed her husband for the first time and stopped struggling against Kammy's grip for a moment. "Kev, what that fuck is going on? Who are these men?"

Lindsay wasn't Irish. She had an almost nondescript accent – one from the home counties. Funny, Smudger had expected her to have come from Essex. Stereotypes eh? She was attractive in a fake kinda way. There was no doubt she'd had some plastic surgery done and her tits were clearly fake, busting to get out of the matching green silk dressing gown. Even without the makeup, Smudger wouldn't mind admitting that he would have a go on her. He'd never been with a bird with fake tits before. But now wasn't the time for that kind of fun.

144

"Hello Lindsay," Smudger greeted her. "I'm dreadfully sorry for the intrusion, but you see your husband had something of mine and well, he didn't play nice. So now I have to leave my calling card. You see," he continued unaffected by the devil's look Lindsay was giving him. "Someone will be along to tidy all this up and I want him to know that it was me who was here. Then I want him to know where to find me next."

He was well-aware of the unhappy look Kammy was giving him and of the confused look Lindsay gave. But the one person he focussed on was O'Conner. He spoke to him now. "Don't worry Kev. I'm not going to harm your wife. I'm not an animal. No, but I am going to damage you. Damage you real bad…"

Gabriel Quinn awoke on Wednesday morning still at his desk. He must have been exhausted to have fallen asleep here. He lifted his throbbing head off the desk and as he stretched, he was reminded that he'd had a tattoo the previous day. Fuck that was sore. He dragged his sorry arse out of the office and down the corridor to the men's locker room where there were showers. He had a locker here with just a towel and spare underwear in it. He sniffed the underwear and was fairly sure they were clean so undressed, grabbed the towel and headed to the open plan shower block. It was 5.30am so he was the only one in here.

Stepping under the scolding water he let it run over his head, letting the hot water stimulate his skin, hoping it would wake him up. Today was not a cold-water shower day. The masking tape that held the cling film over his tattoo went soft and peeled off easily. The tattoo had been bleeding and the hot water stung as it washed away the blood. He gently sponged it down, wincing as he did so. He remained there for a few more minutes before towelling off and grabbing the first aid pack from the wall. He found what he was looking for. The burns pack was simply a roll of cling film which he carefully wrapped round his shoulder using plasters to secure it, so it didn't slip down his arm. Satisfied, he finished dressing in the same faded blue jeans and green polo shirt, made sure he had a lighter and some smokes. He headed for the roof, stopping only at the vending machine to get a coffee.

It was still dark up on the roof and, unsurprisingly, he had it to himself. Taking a long drag on the cigar and blowing the blueish smoke out into the crisp morning he once again turned his thoughts to how he was going to execute his plan. He would be on his own and they would be four. No more he hoped. He had faced worse odds and survived. An inventory of equipment started to form in his head and the plan came together. He was more akin to winging it, but sometimes you needed a plan. Hell, he was smoking a cigar, synonymous with 80's pop culture and 'having a plan.'

Downing the now cooled coffee he lit another cigar and mulled over Detective Godfrey and when to tip him off.

He would do it on the day of the attempted robbery he decided. He didn't want Godfrey having a flash of inspiration and acting before he could finish what he needed to do.

He had been stood there longer than he thought, only roused from his musings by the increased traffic of staff arriving in the car park below him. His watch said 7.45. Christ. He needed to pop back to his office before the 8am briefing that ACU conducted on a Wednesday morning. He could not afford to be late again; Logan was already on his case and that was a shit storm he did not need. He was mostly left alone, just the way he liked it and just the way he needed to keep it. Getting extra attention from Logan was not the way to go about that.

The briefing was just about to begin when he strolled in.

"Nice of you to join us," Logan smirked as he walked into the dull, cream-walled meeting room. There were 5 other members of the ACU present, all of whom nodded greeting to him. He cared little for them but nodded back all the same. He slumped in a chair at the back of the room and switched off. Logan went over the last week and got updates from the five agents. Then there was a knock at the door.

"Enter," Logan called, frustrated at being interrupted.

Constable Cadette opened the door carrying a brown cardboard box in his hands. "Sorry, Guv," he apologised.

"I have a package for one of your team." He handed the box over to Logan and made his excuses and left.

Logan looked at the label on the box and read aloud, confused. "ACU. The one who drives a Rover," Logan looked up, "Anyone?"

'Fucking hell' he thought. He must be the only person here driving a Rover. Surely Logan knew that much about him?

"That'll be me, boss," he said just loud enough to be heard, rising out of his seat.

"Bit cryptic isn't it?" Logan asked quizzically. "Expecting something, Quinn? Car part maybe?"

The other agents laughed heartily.

"I honestly don't know," he admitted taking the package and taking it back to his chair at the rear of the room.

"Well," Logan said, "It will have been scanned when it came in, so it'll be safe, whatever it is. Any other business gentlemen?" He asked the rest of the room. Salman spoke up and he switched off. He read the label and pulled out his small knife to slit the tape open. Folding the cardboard back he found there to be that half shredded packaging paper inside which he pulled out. "Fuck," he exclaimed louder than he intended. All heads turned to look at him, Salman stopping whatever drivel was coming out of his mouth.

"Something interesting?" Logan asked, eyebrows raised

"Err, no guv. Just something from a case. Wasn't expecting it, that's all."

Logan was not going to let it go. "Well, what is it?"

"Um, it's a gearstick," he said honestly

"A gearstick? So it was a car part then!" Logan snorted with amusement at his own wit. The others chuckled at their awkward colleague. He had never really mixed with them and they regarded him as an oddball. An oddball they did not trust.

He didn't answer, electing instead to close the box and stand up. "Will that be all?" He directed the question at Logan who was still laughing. He didn't wait for a reply. "Good, I have work to do." With that he walked out of the room and away to his office.

He shut the door behind him and placed the box on the desk. He could feel anxious sweat forming under his arms. "What the fucking hell," he said aloud, taking his seat behind his sparse desk.

He pondered the box, checking to see if he hadn't missed anything on the outside. There was only brown parcel tape and the address label which was machine printed. He doubted that he would get any prints off the box but made a mental note to get it to forensics anyway.

Carefully lifting the gearstick out of the box, he placed it on his desk in front of him. It was a beautiful piece of manufacturing. The whole thing was chrome. The 4-inch-long stick narrowed at the bottom where it would have led to the main shaft. Working upwards it gradually grew wider, opening up like a blossoming flower.

In the middle of the ice cream cone shaped unit there was set a flat-topped circular chrome button. He figured that it was from an auto gearbox with the button being the selector to take it from park to neutral, to drive and lastly reverse. An auto box selector wouldn't need to have numbers on it unlike a manual stick.

But this one did have a number. It was crudely scratched into the chrome. It was the number 4. Clear as day.

He inspected the rest of the item looking for something else, some other mark or clue. After ten fruitless minutes he resigned himself to defeat. He couldn't see anything on the stick or on the box. "What is that meant to mean?" he asked the room. Unsurprisingly he received no reply.

Chapter 14

"Ah, Rostron, how is the back?" Rowland asked as he sidled up to the evidence desk.

Rostron smiled the warm smile that he gave everyone, splaying his hands as he said, "It still holds me up. I can't complain."

Rowland leant on the evidence room window frame and said honestly, "I don't know how you do it, honestly I don't. I couldn't be here if I couldn't run around and be active." There was no hint of tact in the man's voice whatsoever.

Rostron merely smiled. He knew Rowland was an arsehole, but he knew that despite the way his comments came across, he had not meant to be so thoughtless. That was just his way. Blunt. "Well, ya know, we can't all go waving our guns around can we? The boring stuff still needs to be done."

Rowland paused for a moment, as if he had realised how blunt he had been before shaking the look and pressing on regardless. "Ain't that the truth? You're a better man than I Rostron…"

"What can I do for you?" Rostron interrupted, tired of the game.

Rowland grinned. "I need a van," he said bluntly. "For a case."

Rostron waved down the corridor. "Transport is down on the left. You know that."

Rowland leant in and lowered his voice. "No, sorry, not a marked vehicle. A plain van. Undercover stuff ya see?"

Rostron just looked back at him blankly.

"You have anything in the compound we could borrow Thursday night? I'd have it back with you by morning…"

Again Rostron just stared at him.

"Ah come on, man. Help us out will ya?"

Rostron just wanted rid of the PPO so said, "Fine. There is a blue Peugeot van. Same size as a transit. That any good?"

Rowland stood up straight, grinning widely. "That would be perfect!"

"Fine. I'll leave the keys on the rear wheel tomorrow morning. Make sure its back by Friday morning."

"You," Rowland said pointing at Rostron, "are a fucking diamond. This place wouldn't tick without you."

"Just bugger off will ya? And don't be so fucking condescending." Rostron had had enough.

Rowland held his hands up in mock surrender and backed away. "Thanks again Wilf…"

He slipped his burner out of his pocket and typed into the group chat. *Van and plan is a go. Meet at 11pm outside the Royal Oak tomorrow. I'll be in a blue Peugeot van. It will look like a taxi picking up some lads. Don't be late.*

Quinn was just on his way out of the station, following Rowland who he had seen pestering Rostron. He reminded himself to go ask what it was that he had wanted. That's when his phone buzzed and he ducked away before Rowland clocked him. He didn't look at the screen before answering, too busy trying to watch Rowland. "Yep," He said as way of answering.

"It's Millen," the voice came back.

Suddenly he was all ears. "What is it Millen?"

"You heard of the scrapyard outside of Wokingham called Pistons?"

"Yeah."

"Meet us there."

He shut the call off. Rowland would have to wait.

He pulled into the yard of Pistons and parked his car near an old fire engine and got out. There was blue and white police tape everywhere he looked. He didn't try to begin to understand what had gone on here and instead asked a young PC where he could find Evans and Millen. She pointed in the direction of the tyre shop. He thanked her and lit a cigar and started to walk off towards the tyre shop.

He did not make it five paces before he was stopped in his tracks. Another police car pulled into the yard, but it wasn't one of theirs. It pulled up next to his Rover and out stepped Detective Tabb of Sussex Police. He figured Millen had given her the heads up too. He waited for her to reach him before setting off again. "Tabb, how nice to see you again."

"Under grim circumstances it seems."

"Then you know more than I do."

"It was an assumption."

"Which I imagine is pretty accurate."

They continued on in silence, showing their badges at the entrance to the tyre shop where there was yet more blue and white police tape. They ducked under and saw Evans whom they headed for.

"Detective Evans," Tabb greeted the tired looking cop. "Thanks for the heads up."

154

Evans feigned a smile. "No worries. Glad you could make it. Both of you," he added somewhat restrained.

"What have we got then?" Tabb asked.

"A shit storm, that's what. Crime scene is all over the place. In simple terms, we had a woman in here who was hysterical but unharmed. She's in an ambulance on the way to Royal Berks. In the big fancy warehouse we have a shit tonne of fancy cars and blood. Finally, in the exhaust shop next door we have Mr O'Conner, the owner of this 'ere establishment."

"Let's go talk to him…" Tabb suggested.

"You can try," Millen said as he entered the room, removing a pair of Latex gloves. "But corpses rarely give answers."

"Shit," Tabb breathed.

"Is it O'Conner's blood in the main warehouse?" Quinn asked, cigar hanging from his lip precariously.

"I suppose some could be his, yes, but there is way too much of it. We think it mostly belongs to the three mutilated men that we found dumped in an inspection pit," Millen said.

"Is there anything here specifically for me?" he asked Millen.

"Not that we've found so far, but with the car theme going on we figured it was only a matter of time."

"Thanks," he said begrudgingly.

Tabb interrupted, "So, can you talk us through what you have so far?"

Evans took this one. "Ok, so according to the wife, Mrs Lindsay O'Conner, she was dragged out of her bed by a man who fits the description of one of the perps from the car sales murder. He dragged her down here to this spot where her husband was trapped inside a stack of car tyres…"

"Really?" Tabb asked, incredulous.

"Yup. Weird huh? Anyway, there was another man with him who fits the description of the other perp. It would seem it's the same two guys. So, Lindsay said that they rolled her husband, Mr Kevin O'Conner, through to the exhaust shop…"

"Shall we…?" Millen asked, gesturing for them to follow him.

They all filed out of the tyre shop and ducked under the blue and white tape and into the exhaust shop. In the corner there were some discarded tyres. In front of them was a large sheet with something underneath it.

"Here we have Mr O'Conner," Millen said, "Do you want to see?"

Stubbing out the last of the cigar, much to the disgust of a nearby SOCO, he said, "Of course."

Millen nodded at a woman dressed in a white paper boiler suit. "If you don't mind?"

The woman lifted the corner of the sheet and gently pulled it back.

Tabb heaved, her hand coming up to stop any bile from coming out. "What in God's green earth?"

"Horrible isn't it?" Evans admitted crouching down to inspect the scene a little closer.

"Probably deserved it," Quinn said, emotions devoid from his voice, crouching down next to Evans.

"Really?" Tabb admonished. "Surely nobody deserves *this*."

O'Conner was naked. He was laid on his front on the bare concrete floor, his head and upper body lying in a pool of dark sticky crimson blood that had oozed from a jagged cut in his throat. His hands were tied up behind his back and in turn they were tied to a rope that was looped around his ankles. He was hog tied. But that wasn't it.

Whoever had done this was one sick motherfucker for the murderer had taken the time to insert a car exhaust into the anus of Mr O'Conner. It was like he was some kind of human kebab. None of them wanted to know whether he had been dead or alive when it had happened. Neither did they want to know how far up that exhaust went.

"Any prints yet?" He asked the SOCO.

"This place is a nightmare," she answered. "Prints and grease everywhere. If we get one good print, I'll be amazed."

"I understand. Have you got any gloves?" he asked her. She handed him a box of latex gloves and he pulled a pair on. He started to inspect the body, starting at the toes.

"What are you looking for?" Tabb asked.

"I don't know," he admitted. "But there has be to be something."

Millen, Evans, Tabb and the SOCO all watched as he meticulously went over the corpse. After ten minutes he stood and removed the gloves.

"Well?" Tabb asked.

"Nothing," he admitted, "Although I feel like we're missing something. Let's go see the inspection pit."

Millen led them out of the exhaust shop as the SOCO covered O'Conner back up.

They wound their way through what seemed to be an impressive collection of cars, the smell of oil and grease clogging their nostrils. None of the cops were that into their car heritage so only passed with a fleeting look of curiosity. More blue and white tape sectioned off the corner where the inspection pit seemed to be located. More SOCOs were working this scene in a desperate attempt to photograph, categorise, organise and maintain the integrity of the scene. Detectives rarely helped in this matter. The SOCOs kept wary eyes on the four detectives who ducked under their precious tape. They all peered into the pit.

"Holy mother of God," Tabb exhaled. "What a fucking mess."

The half-exposed inspection pit was a jumble of human body parts. Legs, arms, heads and torsos. There was also a lot of blood. More blood in one spot than you would think possible.

"Not sure I've ever seen anything like that before," Millen agreed, "Are we saying that just two people did this?"

Searching his pockets for his cigars he asked the closest SOCO, "How many are in there?"

A young spectacled man answered without looking up from his clipboard. "We can see three heads…"

"Must have been O'Conner's goons?" Tabb asked rhetorically.

"Killing them is one thing, but to go through the trouble to do this... why? If it's a message, then who's it to?" Tabb suddenly became aware of what she was saying. "Sorry, um, this isn't...?" She tailed off, not wanting to ask the question.

"No," he comforted her, pausing to light a smoke, "This doesn't relate to my brother's death. However, there is a message... or a clue here somewhere."

Millen spoke up. "What makes you say that with any certainty?"

"Because they sent the gear stick to me this morning."

"Why didn't you say?!" Evans butted in, clearly angered.

"I AM saying," he retorted, no time for Evans' petty anger. "It arrived in a box with no markings or clues. The chrome stick itself had only one alteration. It had the number – the digit – four scratched into it."

The other three remained silent until Tabb found her voice again. "I'll ignore the fact that I don't know what gearstick or what incident it relates to despite our agreement. For now I think it's clear that the number has something to do with you, this scene and whatever the fuck these guys are playing at."

"Agreed," Quinn said, nodding. "Shall we fan out? Look round this garage a bit closer?"

Each of them went in separate directions, fanning out over the warehouse in search of… well, they did not know! After 45 fruitless minutes they met back at the pit of death.

"Anything?" Millen asked. They all shook their heads.

Evans raised his hand as if asking for permission to speak. "What if these three are one, two and three, leaving O'Conner as the fourth?"

"What of it?" Millen questioned his partner.

"I don't know… just maybe whatever we're looking for is near that body and not these…"

Tabb spoke up. "That was a much smaller room. You'd think we'd have spotted whatever it was, wouldn't you?"

"Yeah…" Evans began, "But worth another look…"

"Agreed," Quinn said, catching Evans' eye. "We must have missed something. We didn't spend long in there."

"Probably because there is a man with an exhaust pipe up his arse…" Tabb grumbled.

They all filed back out of the car warehouse and over to the Exhaust shop again. They scoured the room, annoying the SOCO no end until they once again admitted defeat.

"What if there's something inside the pipe…?" Evans asked the room.

"Be my guest," Millen gestured to the pipe hanging out of the Irishman's arse.

Tabb grinned and sat back and then exclaimed, "Well lads, I think I've found it!"

All three men looked at her, puzzled. Then they followed her gaze up to the tin roof. She had found it. Written in what appeared to be blood, was a message on the ceiling of the room.

"Fuuuuccckk," Millen and Evans exclaimed in unison.

Quinn read it aloud. "Siblings die but you live a lie."

They all fell silent, each of them digesting the words. It was obviously referring to the massacre of his brother and his family. Only he knew what the lie was about though. Nobody dared ask.

"Is that a clock?" Tabb asked, pointing at the circular image next to the words.

"Looks like it to me," Evans piped up, his neck straining to look up.

Tabb plucked up the courage before the others and asked. "What does it mean though?"

Evans and Millen held their breaths. Even the SOCO held her breath without realising why.

It has to be more than just a dig at me he thought. "We're missing something here. Maybe something to do with the number four?"

They all strained to look back at the ceiling, the SOCO taking photos as they did so.

Millen did his thinking aloud. "What if it's a code of some kind?"

"Using the number four?" Evans chipped in.

"Every fourth letter?" Tabb added.

Millen continued. "So that would give us L, S,B,O,V and I…"

Tabb looked at the three of them. Millen and Evans looked blank. Quinn didn't though.

"What is it?" Tabb asked.

He sighed. Resignation and understanding flooding through him. "I know who it is. I know who's doing this, who had my brother killed."

"Well?" Millen pushed.

"The code. You were right. Every fourth letter. Those letters when put in the correct order spell Bovil's."

"Which is?" Tabb asked, still clueless.

"The bar?" Evans asked

Nodding grimly and perching down on the side of a grimy desk he pulled out his cigars and lit yet another before continuing. "Bovil's the bar. I arrested him there. The only arrest I ever made in that joint. Kinda narrows it down. This was his way of telling me who he is."

The other three exchanged worried looks. "And the clock?"

"Kinda looks like the hands are showing quarter to five, don't they? Or probably more specifically all the fours. 4.44. it's when he wants to meet."

"Jesus. Does he want to get caught?" Tabb asked.

"Where are you going?" Millen asked.

He was walking away now. He did not want anyone else to be involved. He had already told them too much. *Idiot.* This is why he worked alone. He could hear them call after him. "What's his name? Where and when?! Come back!"

He had his head down and was making a beeline for his car. He was not going to stop for anyone. This was his to deal with. He climbed in his car, not daring to look up and started the engine. He wrenched on the steering wheel and wheel-spun his way out of the yard, the car picking up quickly, the tuned engine tearing up the road as he made his escape, fallen leaves kicking up and floating away in his wake.

Chapter 15

"Wooohoooo!" Kammy cried, banging the Beamers steering wheel with unadulterated enthusiasm. "That was fucking awesome!"

Smudger just smiled, looking down at his blood-soaked hands. That had been fun.

"Ah man, the fear. The look of understanding of what was coming plastered all over their faces. Man, it made me feel alive!"

"More than can be said for them!" Both men laughed heartily. They'd left an utter mess behind and much to Kammy's chagrin, a clear and obvious sign for that fucking cop.

"Head for Owusu's," Smudger instructed. "We can get clean clothes and pick up the money. Lay low for the night. Get some beers. Chill the fuck out. Maybe some hookers eh?"

"YEEEEHHAAAAA!" Kammy squealed. With tits and arse on his mind he soon forgot all about the cop and all that his boss was going to jeopardise.

Gilham's office was crowded. She sat at her desk listening to the squabbling going on from the others in her room.

Millen and Evans had returned and started it all. Their report of the scrap yard job was horrific. They had brought a Detective Tabb with them from Sussex Police. Constable Joseph was here as was that idiot Hogan. Finally, sat in the corner just listening was Norgaard, the man MI5 had sent to cast an eye over her man in the ACU. The man most of this arguing was over. She was torn. She wanted him to have his revenge, but that's not what the police was all about, was it? She could not willingly let that happen, especially with Sussex CID and MI5 present. They had to bring the two murderers in, but they needed him to lead them to the perps.

Gilham spoke over the prattling going on in her office. "Have we worked out who these two are yet?"

The room fell silent. Then Joseph spoke up. He was the least senior in the room but had a competence that would take him far, Gilham was sure. "Ma'am, he only made one arrest at Bovil's. Twenty years ago."

"And…" Hogan pressed.

"And his name is Paul Smith or simply Smudger."

"Known associates?" Gilham asked.

"Many," Joseph replied. "And several who fit the profile of the man described by our two witnesses. However, one of these matches left the same prison as Smudger, sorry, Mr Smith, two weeks before he did. His name is Corey Kamara."

167

The room was silent save for the heavy breathing of Hogan.

"Rap sheet?" Gilham asked.

"Both of them were put away for burglary but again both of them were up for manslaughter. It should have been a murder case, but the prosecution botched the job, somewhat suspiciously it appears, and manslaughter was what they faced. Again, amid much suspicion, the main witness went back on their evidence and the case fell apart."

"And this was from the case at Bovil's?"

"Yes, ma'am."

"Thank you, Joseph. Anyone else? Thoughts?"

The room stayed silent until Tabb spoke. "Ma'am, sorry to impose on your force. I'm detective Tabb from Sussex CID. I was at the scene in Pulborough and again at the massacre this morning. We don't know if it's 4.44 am or pm they want to meet or where, but my best guess would be that this Smith wants to face his arresting officer, his self-made nemesis at the place it started. I would say he wants to meet him at Bovil's… if it's still there?"

"It is," Millen confirmed.

"Thank you, Tabb," Gilham acknowledged. "Any advances on that?"

The cops all looked at each other, seemingly glad to have something to grab hold of.

"Seems logical," Evans said finally.

"Very well, Evans, Millen I want you two to set up a surveillance team at Bovil's, specifically covering 4.44. You have the full support of the department. Go." She dismissed the two detectives, with Tabb following.

"Detective Tabb, a moment please," she called, stopping her in her tracks.

"Ma'am," She said, returning to the spot she had been stood.

"Hogan, return to your station and make sure Mahon is briefed."

"Ma'am," he acknowledged, giving Joseph a nasty stare as he left.

That left, Tabb, Joseph and Norgaard.

"You're probably wondering why I've kept you three here."

Tabb and Joseph nodded. Norgaard stayed sat on the leather sofa where he had been the whole time.

"Let me introduce Agent Norgaard. MI5."

Norgaard remained sitting. "Thank you, chief Inspector. While what this Paul Smith has done is obviously horrendous, it is not him that I am interested in. The ACU investigates its own. When it comes to looking at the ACU, that's when we are called in. We have had our eye on Gabriel Quinn for quite some time. He has an excellent record, bringing some high-profile cases in. However, all of these cases have similarities. Their last score has always been stolen from under their noses and they have been arrested for that attempt and for a previous crime. They all describe the same person – the one who steals their score. Who is this person?"

Joseph grimaced. "Are you saying that one of our own…"

Tabb spoke up. "Sorry, is that how you view the ACU here in TVP?"

Joseph looked at her. "Not traditionally, no, but he was one of us. He's had a shit run of it. He's always treated me right." He turned back to Norgaard and continued, "What exactly are you saying Norgaard?"

Gilham was impressed with her constable. He stood up for what he believed was right or wrong.

Norgaard responded in a cool voice, "We believe that he is working with someone. While he does his job in bringing the perps in, he passes the information onto someone else who commits the crime. Probably splits the take."

"You cannot be serious!" Joseph blurted.

"Thank you, Joseph," Gilham calmed.

"Sorry, ma'am," Joseph apologised, blushing.

Tabb re-joined the conversation, "But why?"

Norgaard paused, assessing Tabb. "That we don't know."

Gilham took over. "There is no evidence to suggest that this is the case, although it does look suspicious. Detective Tabb, as an outsider to this force, your thoughts would be appreciated."

Tabb glanced at the constable who had spoken freely in front of his chief. It would appear that this chief, unlike her own, was keen to hear the thoughts of her staff. "I saw nothing in my brief meetings with him. There is clearly a lot of trauma from what happened to him… to his family, but mostly I saw a very competent police officer."

Norgaard stood up. "If you don't mind Chief Inspector, I would like to catch up with Millen and Evans."

"By all means." Gilham waved at the door. "Be my guest. My men will do all they can to accommodate you."

"Thank you." Norgaard nodded his acknowledgement to Joseph and Tabb as he left the room, closing the door behind him.

Gilham looked at the two remaining. "Please, take a seat." she motioned at the two seats in front of her desk. They dutifully sat down.

"Now," Gilham continued. "I don't think anything will go down at Bovil's. I think Smith will want to face him at his brother's house."

"Agreed," Tabb said morosely.

"So why…" Joseph began.

"Why am I putting all my eggs in one basket and focussing on Bovil's?"

"Err, yes, ma'am…"

"Because I trust him, and I believe that sometimes in life we have to ignore… what the justice system dictates and focus on true justice. In this case it is letting him have his revenge on this Smith. Fuck, I shouldn't be saying any of this to you two, I mean, I am the fucking chief!"

Tabb grinned. She liked this Gilham.

Gilham continued. "After all he has been through, maybe, just maybe, this will bring back the old officer I once knew. Lift the cloud of hatred and remorse. That is where you two come in. I have spoken to your chief, Tabb, and you are on secondment to me. You two will stake out his brother's house. Make sure Smith doesn't walk away from this, understand?"

Tabb and Joseph looked at each other in astonishment. Tabb spoke first. "How much involvement do we ha…"

"You are there to make an arrest should there be a living person to arrest. Your main brief is to watch and clear up the mess. Understand?"

"Yes, ma'am," they said in unison.

"I am putting a huge amount of trust in you two. DO NOT let me down."

"No, ma'am" they said, sharing a glance with each other.

"Good, now Joseph, about that other case. Any news?"

"Nothing has come back from any of the detectives I assigned, ma'am."

"Hmmm. Okay. Keep me posted, ok? Although Norgaard will be keeping an eye on Bovil's, he will undoubtedly be interested in the other case what with the same officer being involved an' all."

"Of course, ma'am."

"Sorry to interrupt…" Tabb tried.

Gilham smiled warmly at her. "Joseph will brief you seeing as it has a link to what you are here for."

"Ma'am," Tabb said again.

"Any other questions?"

Both the Constable and the detective shook their heads.

"Very well then. Dismissed."

They both headed for the door when Gilham added. "And Joseph? Ditch the uniform."

"Yes, boss," he acknowledged, holding the door open for the Detective. Then they were gone.

Gilham sat back and rubbed her tired face. "Playing with fire here Karen," she said to herself. Being the chief could be a lonely position. Where was he now? She had called him after being told about his swift departure from the Scrapyard, but he hadn't picked up. She'd tried Shay Logan, his immediate boss in the ACU, but he hadn't heard from him either. Where was he?

Detective Godfrey was an amiable soul. He had been in the thick of the action back in the Eighties when he served in the MET. He had seen it all and had no ideals on going out with a bang. Retirement was four months away and he had great plans. Well, buying a small boat and fishing, that was the plan. He had done more than his thirty years and was looking forward to handing the badge over. Some people were institutionalised. Not him. The job had been wonderful to him, but it was a changing world, and he was a dinosaur. An overweight dinosaur at that!

He reached into the bag of pretzels that sat on his desk and opened the file on his lap. His tweed jacket hung ungainly from his sides and he reached into the breast pocket to fish out his reading glasses. Placing them on the tip of his nose he began to read the file on his assignment. It wasn't one he had wanted but he felt sure there was nothing to find anyway.

He had always liked Ruth. She had been the secretary to the last chief before he left, and now she did an outstanding job for Gilham too. He understood why she had to be looked at, he really did, but he got the sense that as it was him that had been given her to look at, nobody seriously thought she had anything to do with all that money going missing. Then his phone rang.

"Godfrey," he answered, wiping his greasy fingers on his jacket.

"Take a look at who she is dating," said a digitally disguised voice. Then they hung up.

"Hello?" Godfrey said despite the dial tone he could hear. Slowly he replaced the receiver. Who the hell was that? Take a look at who she is dating? Who? Ruth?

He shovelled more pretzels into his mouth and thought. Was that a tip off? How did they know who he was looking at…? It was all very suspicious, but he wasn't one to look a gift horse in the mouth. He picked up his pen in his greasy fingers and wrote on his note pad. Who is she dating? He underlined it twice before turning back to the file. He would finish his cup of tea before he started making enquiries. That was his way.

He could not go back to the station. Not now. Gilham and Logan had tried calling him, but he had ignored their calls.

He sat in a fast-food chain drinking one of their average-at-best coffees. He needed time to think. A lot had happened, and lot was due to go down.

He remembered Smith. Remembered the arrest and the botched case. Smith had been in Bovil's celebrating a big bust with his pals. He'd had the tip-off that he was in there that night so went in after him… to question him about a robbery. Smith hadn't taken kindly to the interruption and a fight had broken out. In amongst the melee where he and his partner had ended up fighting off a bunch of aggressive drunks, Smith had glassed a bouncer. The bouncer later died from his wounds. Smith's case was severely fucked, and he went away for burglary. Someone had gotten to the witness. That was twenty years ago.

Evidently Smith had not forgotten him. Evidently Smith was the one who'd had the attack on his brother and his family. Now Smith wanted to face him.

Well, he was not one to disappoint. But when? Sure, 4.44 am. He got that, but when? Tonight? He would have to prepare for it, just in case. That did not leave much time.

Secondly, where? This was easier. It would be one of two places. Bovil's or his brother's house. Bovil's would be busy tonight. He doubted that was what Rowland wanted.

No, it would be at his brother's house. It was still empty. He had refused to sell it or move into it. That would be where he would want to meet, where he would want to kill him. Fine by him.

Still, he had a contact at Bovil's who he would drop a line to, just to keep an eye out for him in case he was wrong. He imagined that's where Millen and Evans would be anyway.

Then there was the other thing. That was tomorrow night. He had made the call to Godfrey, now he needed to prepare for them. They had the van. He had the skills. A plan had formed. All being well he would make sure they were apprehended and left for the boys in blue while he drove off with a shit tonne of money that would take care of his one true interest for quite some time.

Smudger and Kammy had hidden their beamer in Owusu's garage and gotten cleaned up. It had been a long night and now they were sat in a hot tub drinking champagne with their host.

"Far cry from the bunks," Owusu said. He was a huge man whose parents were from Ghana. His large shiny domed head glinted in the waning autumn sun, water running gently back into the tub. He had done his time at her Majesty's pleasure but now let others get their hands dirty, preferring to profit of the desperation of the weak.

"Ain't that the truth," Smudger said, toasting their host with his champagne. "Thanks for taking us in, Lloyd."

"Don't mention it pal. You paid up front. What could I do? Anyway, happy to help." He laughed deeply, a man in control. "You got any more stashed?"

Smudger could feel Kammy staring at the back of his head, willing him to say nothing. It did not matter to Smudger though. "Yeah, one more. We'll pick it up tomorrow before I go meet him."

"Just you?" Owusu asked, raising an eyebrow.

"Aye, this has nothing to do with Kammy here. He would have earned his money by then. Got plans for it ain't ya?" he added cheerily, grinning at Kammy.

Kammy did not look amused. "Yeah," he said. "I've got plans…" He trailed off before adding. "Lloyd, don't you think that Smudger should just let it go? Ride off into the sunset and enjoy the money?"

"A man's gotta do what a man's gotta do," Owusu announced, toasting Smudger with his glass. "I can respect that."

Kammy opened his mouth as if to continue but thought better of it. He had said his piece more than once now and didn't dare risk saying anything else.

Smudger spoke instead. "I understand your concern Kammy, but my time in the sun will come. I *have* to deal with him first. He took too much from me. He must pay. He must die by my hand. I have seen it in my dreams. I can taste his blood when I sleep at night… "

Even Owusu raised his eyebrows at this but asked, "Do you need anything?"

Smudger regained a little composure. "I'm good thanks, Lloyd. I have my sai. That's all I need."

"Very well. Then I wish you the best of luck in your futures. Until tomorrow, relax, enjoy the food, the champagne and the women." He snapped his fingers and a clutch of women dressed in bikinis came out of the enormous 'conservatory', hips kicking from side to side as they walked. One by one they climbed into the hot tub and began draping themselves over the three men. They quickly forgot any thoughts of money, cars, revenge or tropical retreats.

Thursday morning. 1am. Quinn stood in the living room where once they had shared happy times as a family. With their parents passing away when they were teenagers, the brothers were all they had. Each other.

When his brother Ryan had met Lily, he could not have been happier. He and Ryan were six months from leaving the military at this point and Lily coming along was the perfect tonic for them. A happy and carefree soul to balance out the negativity of the military life.

She had made Ryan so happy and then when they announced they were to have a child; their family was once again more than just the two of them. It made him feel whole again.

He looked around the dark and dirty house. So many happy memories. That is what they were, just memories. Old memories, ones to never be added to. Smith had seen to that. He had brought the family down to just one. Him.

He was stood there now praying that Smith turned up. Praying he showed his face so he could bury those demons. Bury them deep in that animal's face. He had waited a long time for some kind of closure. He doubted it would give him that, but it would feel good all the same.

He sat on a wooden chair that he'd dragged from the dining room and waited.

And waited.

4.44 came and went. He waited until 5.15 before giving up. It was not to be tonight. He would have to repeat this vigil every night until Smith turned up. Fuck. Tomorrow would be a busy night. He needed to tie up the business with Rowland before heading over here to wait. He rose from the chair and left the house. He needed some sleep. It would have to be a whiskey induced one. No way was he falling asleep without it.

Chapter 16

Thursday. 1pm. Owusu's mansion. Lunch. Steak freshly grilled on the BBQ. Smith, Kamara, Owusu and some women.

Thursday. 1pm. Woodley Police station. Lunch. Coronation chicken pre-packaged sandwich. Gilham.

Thursday. 1pm. Flat opposite Bovil's. Lunch. Pizza. Millen and Evans.

Thursday. 1pm. Maintenance van. Lunch. Pasties. Tabb and Joseph.

Thursday. 1pm. Here and there. Lunch. No time. Rowland, Bates, Woody and Bungle.

Thursday. 1pm. His apartment. Lunch. Noodles and Salami. Alone. Alone with his thoughts. A dangerous time. He studied the plan in his head. Legoland would go well, he was sure of it. He knew the four men. Knew their strengths and their weaknesses. He knew the layout. Knew how to handle himself, although he didn't expect it to come to that. Why should it? The trap was set. He just needed to get the job done so he could make it to part two of the night. He had thought about binning off the heist so as to better prepare for 4.44, but those thoughts did not last long. He needed the money for one and secondly, he had been preparing for Smith for nearly 20 years. Of course, he didn't know it was Smith; his dreams and his nightmares always featured a faceless man. Last night was different. Last night the nightmare had a face. Smith was the owner of that face. A face that was going to beg for a mercy that would not be coming.

The countdown was on.

Smudger and Kammy packed up the money into the Mitsubishi Shogun that they had borrowed off Owusu. He would make the Beamer disappear. It would be hot after the scrap yard job and it wasn't worth the risk. They bid their goodbyes to Owusu, promising to meet up again one day. They drove off, heading out to claim the money from the last car.

"I forget, what is the last motor?" Kammy asked, sat in the passenger seat for a change.

"The one I'll keep, that's the one. Owusu got me some new plates for it so it'll be clean."

"I'm no clearer…"

Smudger grinned, childlike excitement shining in his pastel green eyes. "The G20 van."

"Ohhh the A-Team van!" Kammy cooed. Now there is a van worth having. "Does it look the same?"

"Seems to be. Looks like it's been lowered, and they've reconfigured the exhaust to come out the sides. They've also fitted a rock and roll bed in the back, so it'll be ideal for cruising round Europe and keeping out of the cities."

"So, you do plan on getting away after this?"

"'Course. It's not like I'm planning on dying. He's the one who's gonna take his last breath tonight."

Kammy though this over for a while before asking "So where is the G20 now? How are we going to nick it during the day?"

"We're not," Smudger stated matter of fact. "I'm going to buy it."

"You're WHAT?" Kammy almost choked on his can of coke.

Smudger chuckled. "Sorry mate, no killing for you today. I want this van to be clean as it can be, so I'll be buying it with cash. Clean."

"Well, fuck me sideways with a garden fork. What a turn up for the books! What do you need me for then?"

"Once I've got it, we can split the money and you can take this motor and go your own way."

Again, Kammy stayed silent. Then said, "And you're ok with that?"

"Yeah man. I've enjoyed your company, but we've been together for twenty bloody years man! Time to go our separate ways…"

"I mean, you don't want help…"

"I know what you meant Kammy. Like I said, this is personal."

"He put me away too…"

"This is true, but I'm the one who can't let it go. You're a better man than I. Move on mate. Let this idiot deal with his revenge, ya feel me?"

Kammy crossed his arms. He *didn't* want to get involved with the revenge killing, but he did kinda feel left out. "If that's what you want, boss…"

They drove on in silence towards the last stash which sat in the retirement capital of the South, Worthing.

Quinn dressed in alternative clothes. Black combat trousers over black tactical boots, laced up tight. He shrugged on a black base layer, being careful not to remove the sticky tape that held the cling film on over his now very sore tattoo. He then pulled on a tactical gilet. He called it tactical, but really it was a modified fisherman's waistcoat. The pockets were handy for storing his numerous tools and he had lined the jacket with Kevlar sheets to give him some protection. In the early days he had taken some beatings and with the kids all carrying knives and guns these days, he couldn't be too careful. He strapped on his leg holster for his Rambo-esque knife and lastly slipped on his trusty Black baseball cap. Backwards obviously. He hadn't shaved for a week now, so the beard was starting to take over, giving him a grizzly, menacing appearance. Your average law breaker would think twice about having a go.

He picked up the keys to his blacked out pickup truck that sat under a cover in a lockup that he rented. The sun had set already on the cold October night. Some fireworks had already started to go up, crashing and banging like a woefully out of sync orchestra.

He had hours to go until the hit, but he wanted to pass by Ryan's house first and leave a few items in readiness for the showdown. Would Smith come alone? He figured that he would but wanted to be prepared for more.

The pickup started first time and roared into life, the modified V8 rumbling satisfyingly, an ozone polluting vapour trail swirling away in the crisp air. He revved the huge engine, the chassis twisting under the huge torque. Briefly smiling to himself, he put the truck in gear and pulled away.

"You think it'll happen tonight?" Millen asked Evans. They were alone in the empty apartment that looked out over Bovil's. Norgaard had promised to return later in the evening. said he had a few things to work out first.

"The question is, will it happen here?" Evans countered.

"What do you mean?" Millen queried, sipping his umpteenth coffee of the day.

"Well, this is only one possibility isn't it? What if they plan on meeting somewhere else?"

"Like where?"

"What about at this brother's house?"

Millen thought this over. "Why didn't…"

"Only thought about it today. I hear that he never sold his brother's place. It sits empty. What if it's there that this goes down?"

Millen stared at his partner. "Have you told Gilham?"

It was Evans turn to lower his binoculars and stare at his partner. "No… Do you think we should?"

They looked at each other for a long moment. They owed him nothing, but something compelled them to agree to leave that information out. Silently nodding agreement Evans went back to his binoculars and Millen stretched out on the reclining plastic sun lounger they had brought for the job.

The van was cramped, so it was lucky there was only the two of them in there. Tabb and Joseph had filled the time with small talk in-between napping on the small piece of sponge they called a bed. They had run out of youthful anecdotes, discovering in the process that their fathers had worked together on an oil platform off the Scottish coast some years ago. Both now seemed to be avoiding what they both actually wanted to talk about.

Tabb broke the silence from her position on the mattress. "You think it'll be tonight?" She asked nonchalantly.

"I do," Joseph said flatly.

"Why?" Tabb asked suddenly intrigued in this Constable's reasons.

"There can't be much more money for them to gather can there? There are no reports of any killings or thefts last night which indicates to me that the time has come to get that revenge…"

Tabb thought about this for a minute before replying. "And if it is tonight, what will you do?"

"Hang on," Joseph interrupted her. "Sorry, a pickup just pulled onto the drive."

Tabb clambered up off the mattress and leaned over the seats where Joseph sat, pretending to read a newspaper. "Is it Quinn?"

"I've never seen that truck before…" Then, as the figure clambered out of the cab. "But that sure looks like him. I mean, the profile, the way he moves…"

"You sound like you have a crush on the man."

"You know what I mean," Joseph snapped, irritated.

"Alright, alright… shit. He just looked straight at us!"

It was true, the man dressed all in black stared straight at the van. They couldn't make out his face, the streetlight outside the property was inconveniently out. He was probably looking at the van with suspicion, the fake decorator's logo seemingly doing little to convince him it was there legitimately.

"Wrong time of day for us to be sat here," Tabb whispered.

"Yeah, not that well thought out was it?" Joseph whispered back.

They sat in silence as the figure gave up staring and moved to the side of the house and disappeared down the side.

"What do we do?" Tabb asked

"Nothing. Make a note of it and see what happens."

Rowland drove the Blue Peugeot van at the speed limit, his eyes flicking this way and that, scanning for anything out of place. Bonfire night was always an odd evening. The usually dark skies become lit with brightly coloured explosions accompanied by the 'ahhhs' and 'oooohs' of the people watching in fascination. As a child he had himself loved bonfire night. The candy floss, the staying up late, the fireworks. These days it meant very little and if anything, the crack of the fireworks put him on edge slightly. The sounds were sometimes a bit too close to the sound of gunfire.

But by 11pm the explosions were starting to diminish, with only those who were flirting with the law still sending fireworks up. Mostly it was now just the remains of the bonfires. The roads were moderately busy with people returning from gatherings and the odd passing fire engine no doubt attending a bonfire that had gotten out of control. He pulled into the car park of the Royal Oak at 10.55 just as a taxi was leaving. Stood there was Woody. Rowland pulled into a space near the fence and the overhanging trees. Woody walked over to the van and knocked on the window.

Rowland buzzed the window down. "Did you just get out of that taxi?" he asked angrily

Woody looked taken aback by the angered question. "Well yeah, I don't have a car…"

Rowland could have throttled him. "What if the taxi driver had seen this van pull in. What if he thought it was odd that you were dropped off here at closing time? What if he reads a report in a few days about the heist and the sighting of a blue Pug van?! Then what? Tell me you didn't have him pick you up from your place?"

Woody's face told a story that he didn't want to share. "No, no... he picked me up from outside the Tattoo parlour..."

"That's even worse!" Rowland growled. "Why do you have to be such a fucktard? This job better be worth it."

Woody latched onto this lifeline, ashamed of his own incompetence. "It sure will be, boss. No worries. Be a huge haul..."

"Just get in the fucking van, you tool."

Woody hung his head, circled the van and climbed into the passenger seat. "Where are the other boys?"

"They'll be here. Just not as fucking obviously as you that's all."

They waited for ten minutes in silence before they saw Bungle and George emerge from the pub. Bungle pulled his phone out of his pocket and made a call while George lit a cigarette next to him.

Rowland's phone rang. "Yeah?" He answered.

"Alright, boss. It's Josh. Taxi for two outside the Royal Oak please mate."

"No worries," Rowland said into the phone before hanging up. "You see," he said to Woody. "Simple ain't it? Nobody would question them, would they?"

Woody shrank deeper into his seat. "Sorry, boss," was all he could manage.

They sat in silence for another few minutes and when they saw Jamie stub out his cigarette Rowland started the van and circled round to pick the other two up. Woody took the unspoken hint and clambered into the back while Jamie and Josh climbed into the front seats.

"Boys," Josh said as a way of greeting. "We all ready?"

Rowland put the van into gear and pulled off. "Fellas. Everything is in place. Dipshit back there assures us this is a big score. This should be nice and clean. In and out. All the gear is in the back. We'll go find a nice quiet spot and go through the plan, gear up and get our game faces on. Capeesh?"

"Fuck yeah!" The two old heads cheered.

The van pulled out of the car park and into the night.

It was gone midnight when he left his brother's old house – much later than he had intended and climbed back into his pickup. He would have to put his foot down now to get to Legoland and into position. Reversing off the drive he glanced in his rear-view mirror at the painter's van parked on the other side of the road. Talk about incompetence. It was blatantly a surveillance team although he had been unable to make out who exactly was in the van. It mattered little to him. If they hadn't come over to see him, he guessed this was a team dispatched by Gilham to keep an eye on him. He would put good money on there being a team outside Bovil's too. Probably in one of those flats opposite he imagined. He pulled away and out of the road without another look back. They weren't going to follow him.

In the van, they watched. They saw him drive off, but they didn't follow. That wasn't their brief although Tabb clearly thought they should go after him.

"He'd clock us in no time," Joseph said. "He would have noted the van even if he didn't think it was a cop van."

"Still…" Tabb tailed off

"Look, how about we let Gilham know? That make you feel better?"

Tabb brightened up. "Yeah, that really would."

"Fine." Joseph dialled Gilham's number. She picked up straight away. Did she ever switch off from the job? "Guv. Thought you should know. We've just seen what looked like him arrive at his brother's house in a black pickup truck. He was in the house for an hour. He just drove off again."

"You sure it was him?"

"Can't be 100 percent," Joseph admitted. "We couldn't see his face and I don't recognise the truck. Its plates didn't match the vehicle either. But he moved like him you know? Seemed to know the gaff too…" Joseph tailed off, not knowing what else to say. Not *wanting* to say anything else.

"Good work Constable. You and Tabb holding up okay?" She asked.

"Yeah, all good here, boss."

"Good. Hang around. Stay alert at Four Forty-Four."

"Gotcha, boss." With that he heard Gilham hang up.

"Well?" Tabb asked

"Stay put basically."

Tabb climbed into the front seat next to Joseph and folded her arms in silence. She was not best pleased, that much Joseph could tell.

What to do with that information? Gilham thought to herself. She sipped at the glass of wine that she cradled in her hand. Alone in her house as she always was bar the odd appearance of one of her cats, she flicked through the numbers on her phone. Call him? Call Norgaard? She knew she should. But he would have wanted him tailed and Gilham had not instructed Tabb or Joseph to do such a thing. She knew he would be pissed at her. She tapped the green phone symbol anyway. She had to follow the book at some point, hadn't she? It rang four times before Norgaard picked up.

"Norgaard," he said.

"It's Gilham. We think we saw him leaving his brother's old property. He was in a black pickup truck. Plates didn't match and it's not a positive ID but my team on the ground said the man moved like him and seemed to know the property."

"Did they follow him?"

She knew he would ask. "No. That was not their brief."

"Why the hell not?!"

She sighed inaudibly. "He would have clocked the van straight away. They could never have followed him…"

Norgaard cut her off, "And you didn't have another team round the corner ready to follow?"

"No. I didn't. No resources…" Again, Norgaard cut her off.

"I'm sorry, Chief Inspector. That is not good enough. You should have asked me. I expected better of you. Any idea of where he is heading?"

"No, but we'll know if he turns up at Bovil's…" Once again Norgaard cut her off. She was really starting to dislike this agent.

"I'm heading there now anyway. Please keep me informed Inspector."

Then he hung up. "Prick," she said aloud stroking the ginger cat who had jumped up onto her lap. "Men eh, Alan?" she asked the cat. She got fur in her wine glass as an answer.

Chapter 17

Quinn drove up the winding road that led to the theme park entrance. He passed the overflow car parks at the far extremes of the vast land and continued up past character statues and welcome signs towards the main car parks. He knew they would have CCTV, but he didn't much care. The trucks plates were fake, or at least duplicates of a SORN car somewhere and he planned on wiping the CCTV drives before he left. So he continued on past car parks E, D and C. He chose car park B because from previous visits he knew there were corner spots at least partly hidden by overhanging trees. He reversed into one such spot, nose facing out just in case he needed a quick getaway. Old habits.

Making sure the truck was locked he started off towards the main security gate for the back offices, pulling on tactical gloves as he went. The public gate was off to his right as he walked briefly back down the hill before taking a right turn signposted 'Lego HQ. Staff only'.

He walked along this path, the main office buildings rising up from behind, more character statues and a lone security barrier with a small booth. This is where his man would be sat right now. Maybe even watching his arrival with what he hoped would be a smidge of suspicion.

He reached the small booth and found a man in his late twenties watching something on his phone. He hadn't even noticed him arrive at the booth. He knocked on the glass window. The security guard almost hit the ceiling he jumped so hard. "Fuck is this?!" He exclaimed in a thick Polish accent. He hadn't even reached for his radio. This wasn't America. He didn't carry a gun. Not even mace or a baton. Sometimes the security at British places was woefully inept.

"Good morning," he said, trying to keep the moment light. "I'm here to take watch for a while."

The man looked completely bewildered. He searched for the right words. "Who are you?" He managed.

"Diamond security. Same as you." He flashed a fake badge at the security guard. "With the big takings from tonight's fireworks, they sent me along to double the numbers."

The guard looked visibly confused but had relaxed after seeing the badge of the company he worked for. "No one told me," he pointed out.

"Typical," he said as if knowing what jackasses Diamond Security could be. "Well, I'm here now. You can go take a break if you want..." he managed to read the name badge. Szczesny. How the fuck do you pronounce that?! "Err, sorry, how do you pronounce your name?"

"Shez-nay. Woy-check shez-nay. You English have trouble with my name always. It is not difficult." He seemed genuinely annoyed.

"Okay then Woy-check. Go take a break. I've got this covered for a while. Go chill out mate."

Szczesny looked uncertain but eventually opened the door to the vestibule, picked up his phone and stepped out. A modicum of professionalism came over him just then when he asked. "How come you no in uniform?"

He smiled. Good lad. "I'm sorry Woy-check. But this is for your own good." With that, he swung a huge right hook, clubbing the Pole square on the temple. His eyes rolled to the top of his head and went down like a sack of shit. He caught him on the way down, not wanting the innocent man to hurt himself when crashing to the ground. "Gotcha," he said to the unconscious man who was now half cradled in his arms. He stood up, hefting the Pole up from under his arms and began dragging him towards the main buildings. He had fifteen minutes before the cash transfer truck arrived.

He used the security fob on the young man's wrist to buzz them into the building where he found the nearest office and dumped the Pole into a seat. He quickly stripped the uniform off him, stripped off his own clothes and donned the Diamond Security uniform of navy-blue trousers and pale blue shirt that featured pointless epaulettes. He made sure to remove the security fob from his wrist and placed the Diamond Security baseball cap on his own head, this time with the peak facing forward. Lastly, he used a cable tie to cinch the man's wrists behind his back and around a desk leg. He took out some gaffer tape from his small rucksack, placed a strip of tape over the half-naked man's mouth and then stuffed the roll of tape and his clothes back into the bag.

Backing away from the young man he said. "Sorry again buddy," and walked out of the office, closing the door behind him. Job one done. He quickly made his way back to the booth and sat down. Now he waited.

Rowland pulled off the main road and up the hill that led to the park's entrance and drove into car park D, halfway up the hill. He looped the van round and came to a stop to the left of the car park entrance and shut the engine and lights off. From here they would be able to see the van head up the hill, but the van's occupants wouldn't see them. Perfect.

"Game faces boys," he said to the other three in the van. They'd swapped the baseball caps for rubber masks. With Halloween having just passed there were a plethora of masks readily available. Each of them wore a different mask, but all of them covered their faces completely, totally concealing who they really were. They sat in silence, waiting for the payday to come up the hill.

Marcus Bent and Carl Asaba had been working together for the last two years. They enjoyed their job, mostly because they had a right laugh together. Of similar age and with shared interests the shifts always passed quickly. Tonight's shift was overtime for the pair as the theme park usually had pick-ups during the day, but with the fireworks takings the park had requested an extra pickup.

"You ever been to the park as a guest?" Marcus asked

Carl was driving this evening. They took it in turns to drive the big metal box and conversely took it in turns to be the runner. "Nah, you? Reckon I'm too old for this place now. Back when I was a kid I would have killed to come here though."

"Yeah, we came here last summer," Marcus replied looking out the toughened glass window at the wizard statue they passed at the entrance to the park. "Brought Denny here for his birthday last year. It's actually a pretty cool place. I mean, the rides are for kids, but the setup of the place is awesome man. Busy though. Like, really fucking busy!"

"I couldn't do with the queuing mate. Fuck that."

"Fair enough. You'll change your tune when Michelle and you start producing little ones."

"Do one Marcus!" Carl joked. "I ain't ready for kids. Neither is she. Got a life to live first, ya know? Besides, my football career would come to an end…"

"Career?!" Marcus burst into laughter. "We play Sunday league football mate. You can't call that a football career!"

"Why not?" Carl demanded as the van climbed the hill, passing car park D without noticing the parked Peugeot van.

Marcus continued to laugh. "Anyway, who we playing this week, do ya know?"

Carl thought for a moment. "It's a cup match, I think. Some team called Gatwick Blades. Scotty P said they're crap though. Lose every week apparently."

"Awesome. I feel a hat-trick coming on!"

"Dream on son!"

They approached the security booth and the red and white barrier that blocked their way.

"Wonder if the poor schmuck is even awake," Marcus quipped as Carl came to a stop at the barrier. The man in the booth had his head down looking at his phone, baseball cap pulled down low.

"Alright mate, here to pick up the shit load of cash they took this evening."

He didn't look all the way up, unwilling to let his face be seen. "No worries fellas. You know the drill. Go right on through," he tapped the button to raise the barrier which slowly made its way to the vertical in front of the security van.

"Quiet night?" Carl asked.

"First people I've seen since the late shift manager left," he replied as jovially as he could while keeping the air of boredom his position should evoke.

"Same place as usual?" Carl asked, slightly amused by the somewhat shy guard.

"Yeah, same as usual." He tapped his phone as if the two men were keeping him away from something important.

The barrier was all the way up now. Carl shook his head in mock disgust at the guard. "Cheers then," he said sarcastically, driving away.

Marcus laughed once they were out of earshot. "Well he was weird!" they both laughed heartily. "Imagine being stuck in the van with that fella all day!?" Carl said.

"Better than you, ya boring twat!" Marcus boomed, donning his helmet.

Carl looked genuinely hurt. "Fuck you man! Jog on will ya so we can get outta here."

The van drove round the back of the office buildings and reversed up to the electronic shutter. Marcus tapped the remote they had been given and the shutter began to rise. The cash office and collection point were in a different building to the one where Szczesny now laid unconscious. The park kept the visitors block very separate from the cash offices due to the enormous amounts of money that came through the gates. Sure, most of the entrance fees were paid on cards but once in the park people still used a huge amount of cash. Food, beverages, fairground style attractions like basketball throwing or yellow duck fishing. That's not even including the plethora of shops selling themed gifts and clothing. Oh yes, this was a money-making machine.

Once the New Road Security van disappeared out of view Rowland started the Peugeot van up and crept out of the car park.

"Shouldn't we knock the headlights off?" Bates asked the boss.

"Damned auto lights, aren't they?"

Slowly heading up the hill so as not to catch the NRS van at the barrier they all prepared themselves for the task ahead. They all knew the plan. Now was the time to execute and not fuck up.

"As soon as we get to the booth, you're outta here ok?" Rowland said to Bungle.

"I've got this," Josh said, slightly muffled by the clown mask he wore.

They turned the last corner and saw the barrier coming down. 200 metres further up they could see the back end of the NRS van turning right behind a building.

"This is it!" screeched Zippy excitedly.

"Shut it Woody!" cursed Rowland as he brought the van to a hurried stop at the barrier. No sooner had the van stopped, the side door flew open and a clown faced man leapt out.

Rowland didn't wait to see what happened next, instead flooring the van and crashing through the barrier and after the NRS van.

Once the shutter raised the full distance Carl reversed the truck into the loading bay where two employees were waiting for them. These two were tasked with the transfer of the bags of money. Each bag had been totalled up and a label attached. This label digitally held the details of the contents and would allow NRS to scan the bags in making sure there was no way the two parties could argue over any discrepancies.

"Bang on time as usual," Sheila Dearden said tiredly. Her auburn hair was hastily tied up in a bun on the top of her head, showing off large silver hooped earrings that nearly touched her shoulders. Although only 32, the years of raising three children on her own had taken its toll, the crow's feet and tired eyes making her look much older.

"You'll be sat at home cradling that glass of wine before you know it," Graham Benstead replied cheerily. Graham was the polar opposite of Sheila. He was in his late forties, never married and a serial traveller.

"And you'll be sat on that plane doing the same before you know it!" Sheila remarked somewhat jealously, "Where is it that you're going this time?"

"Vietnam and Cambodia. Going to rent a motorbike and travel up the coast before flying to Cambodia to see Angkor Wat," Graham enthused.

They watched as the van backed up to the loading platform where they stood and the man they recognised as Marcus clambered out of the passenger door. "Evening guys!" He called cheerily. He had no sooner got out of the van when they heard the screeching of tyres and the revving of an engine. All three of them turned and gawped as a blue Peugeot van came hurtling into the bay. The van lurched forward as the driver slammed the brakes on. It came to a halt partly assisted by the front of the NRS van which it had bumped into. The impact was enough to slam Carl back into his seat before the momentum threw his head forward again and into the steering wheel. He was, at least for the moment, out cold.

Rowland, Woody and Bates all jumped out of the barely stopped van, bringing their Sig MCX semi-automatic firearms to their shoulders. "Nobody move!" bellowed Rowland. "Get your hands in the air!"

Graham and Sheila thrust their arms into the air, fear written all over their faces. Marcus hesitated, resulting in more shouting. "I said hands UP!" Rowland screamed. Was it fear that had gripped this man? thought Rowland as he moved closer to the security van runner, his weapon aimed square at the man's face. Maybe it was a dash of heroism or sense of duty. Whatever it was, it was dumb.

Rowland was now just feet from Marcus and still he had not raised his hands. For the record, it was fear that had frozen Marcus. That fear cost him a broken nose, Rowland turning his weapon round and smashing Marcus in the face with the butt of his gun, sending blood bursting out across the floor. Sheila let out a gasping scream. "Shoulda put your hands up or your visor down son," Rowland said as the man crumpled to the floor holding his face, blood pouring out from between his fingers.

"Alright you two," Rowland said to Graham and Sheila. "Get over there and face the wall," he indicated with his weapon where they were to go, "Don't be no heroes here. Do as I say, and everyone gets to go home tonight." Graham and Sheila unsteadily and slowly moved towards the wall indicated by the man with the burnt face rubber mask.

Marcus was still sat on the floor nursing his bloody nose. He could not quite believe what was happening. It all happened so fast. The training videos they watched said it would be quick and shocking. They were right. Is Carl ok?

he thought through the grogginess. He was aware of someone yelling and then saw the two employees with their arms in the air moving towards the wall off to his left. He thought he recognised them. Sheila maybe? He couldn't remember the man's name. Then there was more shouting. The angry yelling got closer to his muffled ears and closer still. He began to be able to make out words. "Up!" "Don't… around…"

"Get up!" Bates was yelling at Marcus. "Don't you fuck around. Get up!!"

Marcus tentatively dragged himself to his feet, one hand still covering his bleeding nose. "Get over there with the others!" He heard the man scream. Was he wearing a rubber mask? Some kind of goblin? Carefully he made his way to the wall and stood next to the two park employees. He smeared the wall with blood where he put his hands against it.

Rowland turned to Woody and said "Zippy. Start loading those bags of cash into our van."

"Will do, boss," he said, dropping his weapon to his side so it was hanging from its shoulder strap. He moved over to the stack of bags and whistled. This was a fucking good stash!

Quinn saw the van coming. It was hard not to. They had their bloody headlights on! He watched it pull up and saw the man jump out. This was clearly the man who was supposed to silence the security guard.

He noted the weapon the man was bringing up to his shoulder, leaning in to line his eye up with the sight. It was a Sig MCX. Idiots. Even using the weapons that they used at work. The 5.56 Carbine was a weapon brought in after he left the military, but he had played with it in the shooting range. Firing up to 900 rounds a minute it could be a thirsty weapon, but it was fairly compact. Not a bad weapon, but not one he would choose to use.

He also clocked the Glock 17. The 17 round sidearm was a weapon he had trained with relentlessly when he was in the military. It was a solid weapon. Reliable. Robust.

The man, he guessed by his size and build that it was McEachran, moved smoothly and quickly. Szczesny wouldn't have stood a chance. He was different though. McEachran was good, but he was better. Police training vs elite military training. There was only one winner.

"Move and I'll shoot!" McEachran screamed at him. Too late. He was on the move. He ducked down to his left out of immediate sight and drew his knife from its sheath where he had placed it on top of his rucksack. Because the booth was small, the door opened outwards and, on his haunches, he burst out of the door just as the trigger happy McEachran opened fire on the booth.

Idiot. He would have put good money on Rowland expressly forbidding opening fire on anyone during the hit. Nobody needed that kind of heat.

Maybe it was frustration on McEachran's part. It was well known that the police hardly ever got to use their weapons. The paperwork and subsequent removal from live fire duty for six months was something that he knew these guys loathed. Maybe this was him getting the kicks he had hoped he would get at work.

Whatever the reason, he was laying waste to the booth with the MCX. Continuous loud cracks roared from the Carbine and the booth was peppered with holes that soon turned the thin metal booth into a shredded mess.

McEachran was not messing around. Fucking idiot. He heard the gun click, reminding the clown faced man that his weapon was out of ammo.

This was his moment. Quinn launched himself at the dirty cop. From his low-down position his powerful quads and hamstrings burst into being, firing him up and towards McEachran. He imagined the startled look that was behind the mask. He smiled inwardly. Nobody would have predicted a for-hire security guard to attack. No way.

He used his shoulder to knock McEachran off balance, simultaneously grasping the MCX and forcing it away out of Mceachran's grip. If he hadn't been wearing a mask the shock would have been written all over his face. The momentum of the attack sent McEachran falling backwards but was immediately catapulted back towards his attacker as he wrenched on the MCX. McEachran was dragged forwards from the shoulder strap straight into the rising elbow that was coming his way. The elbow crashed into McEachran's chin, knocking his head back savagely.

He quickly swiped with his knife and cut the strap that held the automatic weapon. McEachran had a strong chin. The elbow blow would have knocked most men clean out. The dirty cop however was groggy but not out. Stumbling backwards he shook his head to clear his juggled brain and his eyes regained focus. He instinctively grasped for his sidearm.

He saw it coming though and again launched himself at McEachran, not giving him the space to draw the weapon. Throwing the MCX to one side he grabbed the right hand of McEachran and stopped him from drawing the gun. As he did so he drew back his shoulders, tensed his neck and head butted his assailant square on the nose, breaking it instantly.

This second blow did knock him out. He went down heavily, and he made no attempt to catch him, letting him fall to the ground with a solid thud.

Wasting no time, he grabbed McEachran from the ankles and dragged him to the back of the shredded booth. He grabbed the cable ties from his bag and hog tied the unconscious man. Hands and ankles bound together then linked at the small of his back, he wasn't going anywhere.

211

He ripped the mask off him and revealed his bloody face to check the identity of his attacker. Good. It was McEachran. Now he knew who he would be dealing with at the vans.

Quickly donning his tactical vest, slipping a new clip into the MCX he set off at a sprint towards the cash office.

Woody picked up four bags, two in each hand and walked them gleefully from the pile to the Peugeot. He opened the rear doors and threw the cash-laden bags in the back and then went back for more. Meanwhile Bates was cable tying the hands of the three prisoners while they stood against the wall. Rowland still had his weapon up and concentrated on their backs. He wasn't taking any risks. He watched Woody shuttling bags of cash back and forwards from the pile to the van.

Maybe this will be the last hit, he thought absentmindedly. Woody was an idiot, but he had come up trumps with this one.

Then a thought occurred to him. What if the van had done some pickups before this? What if the NRS van was half full already? If this was going to be his last hurrah, why not make it a really good one?

Seeing that Bates had completed his task of tying the three up he lowered his weapon and sidled up to the NRS runner.

"What's your name son?" he asked. He was greeted with silence. "I asked," he said, shoving the man in the back, "What is your name?"

"M… M… Marcus. Marcus Bent," the runner stammered.

"Okay Marcus," Rowland continued. "How do I get in your van?"

Marcus paused for a minute considering the question and what his options were here. He settled on. "You can't."

"Never tell me 'you can't' Marcus. We both know that's a lie."

Marcus seemed thrown. It wasn't strictly a lie. "You… you can't. I can't. I mean, the driver has to let you… or I, in."

"That's more like it. See, that's what I wanted to know. Now, tell him to let you in."

Marcus turned his head to half look at the man who questioned him and to cast a glance at the van where Carl sat. If Carl was okay, then he would have activated the alarm meaning the police would be here soon. "He won't do it," he stammered. "It's against policy."

Rowland laughed. "Of course it's against policy. You're being robbed!" he grabbed Marcus by the collar and led him towards the NRS van. It was soon clear to both men that carl was still out cold.

"Shit," they both said, Rowland louder than Marcus.

Rowland shoved the cable-tied man towards the van and demanded. "Wake him up and get me in that van!"

Marcus stumbled but managed to stop himself from falling. He shouted. "Carl! Carl! Wake up buddy! Are you okay? It's Marcus, mate. We need your help. Wake up!!" In desperation and with his wrist tied, he tentatively head butted the door window, acutely aware of the broken nose he was sporting. He continued to shout at his friend while the scarecrow-faced man shuttled the cash bags to their van. "Come on man! Wake UP!!"

This seemed to get through, and Carl came to with a jolt, hurriedly looking around, unsure of his surroundings. Rowland quickly grabbed Marcus. He dropped his MCX to his side and drew the Glock from its leg holster and brought it up to Marcus' temple.

"Don't even think about that panic button, Carl!" he yelled, grabbing the attention of the driver before he could compute what was going on. "Hit that button and your buddy here dies. We already have a shit load of money, so him dying isn't the end of the world for us. BUT his death will be on your conscience. So, do the right thing and open the door will ya?"

Carl quickly came to his senses seeing his buddy with a gun to his head. How did this happen? How did it all go south so quickly? What was he meant to do? They were told to never open the van to an attacker, but that was his

214

friend with a gun to his head. He would not let Marcus die.

"Don't shoot!" Carl cried out desperately throwing his hands into the air in surrender.

Rowland pressed the muzzle of his Glock harder into Marcus' temple.

Marcus instinctively tried to move his head away from the cold steel and said to his friend. "Carl. Mate. Open the door, okay?"

Carl nodded and slowly moved to press the door release button. "I'm going to open the door, okay?" he said as if to confirm to the man with the gun what he was doing. "Just don't shoot Marcus."

The passenger door clicked open. "Zippy!" Rowland called. "Get the man out of the van will ya?" he kept the Glock pressed hard into the side of Marcus' head.

Woody circled round to the passenger door, his MCX raised. He didn't move smoothly like the others. This was the first time he'd even held a gun. He used his left hand to open the door fully and beckoned Carl to get out, needlessly screaming. "Get out of the van, fucknuts!"

Carl still had his hands raised and nodded his understanding, slowly shuffling over to the open door. He stepped out, hands still raised and looked at Woody expecting more instructions.

"Move!" Woody screamed. "Over with the others," he added a little less hysterically.

Carl dutifully started a slow walk towards Graham and Sheila. "If the van is still for too long HQ will alert the police. You don't have long," he said helpfully.

"Was that a fucking threat?!" screamed Woody. "Have you activated the alarm?"

"No! No, of course not. I was just saying…"

CLICK!

Woody pulled the trigger of his weapon. Nothing happened. He squeezed the trigger again, the weapon aimed at the head of Carl. Again, nothing happened. "What the fuck?!" Woody exclaimed confused. Did he have the safety on or something?

Then Rowland spoke up. "Do you really think we'd give you a loaded weapon?" he asked incredulous at the man's stupidity.

Woody looked at Rowland in bewilderment. "I don't have any ammo?" he asked dumbfounded.

"Of course not, you fucking retard. What you just did proved how right I was too. Why were you going to kill him, huh? Do you understand the shit storm that would be brought down on us if you'd killed him?"

Woody's body language gave away his fleeing bravado. "But… but… It sounded like he'd activated the alarm…"

"But he didn't, did he? He just said what would happen. He explained but you didn't listen. Too excited. Too trigger happy. You're done after this. No more jobs." Rowland spoke with a finality that stopped Woody from even saying another word.

Woody shoved Carl in the back with his unloaded weapon. Carl did as he was told, just thankful to still be alive. He leaned against the wall next to Marcus and Bates cable tied his wrists.

"George," Rowland called. "Keep an eye on those three. Zippy, continue to load the cash. I'm gonna check the inside of the van." His two masked accomplices nodded understanding and he climbed into the van. Inside he stepped behind the front seats and into the back where he discovered around fifteen boxes like the ones they use to collect cash from banks and shops. Bingo.

CRACK!

His greedy little thoughts were disturbed by the report of a shot ringing out, the sound bouncing off the walls of the loading bay like a squash ball striking the walls of a court. What the fuck!?

Quinn had finished his sprint just in time to hear Woody be reprimanded by Rowland. From what he could make out, they hadn't given Woody any ammo and he had tried to use the gun. He pulled the mask that he'd taken from McEachran over his face and glanced down at the MCX in his own hands, glad that there were bullets in his.

Peeking round the corner of the loading bay entrance he could see a woman and two men stood against the wall at the far end. Woody was now leading a man dressed in the NRS uniform to stand next to his colleague. There was blood smeared on the wall, seemingly from the NRS man who already stood there. The one who he assumed was Bates cable-tied the new arrivals hands together before Rowland spoke. He watched Rowland climb into the van.

So, they had managed to get access to the van eh? Wanted a bigger score. That greed wouldn't be why they failed tonight, but it sure made his job easier. Once Rowland had disappeared from view, he made his move. He edged round the corner and raised his weapon. He took aim and fired.

CRACK!

The bullet travelled at 914 metres a second. Bates was stood fifteen metres away. From the moment that he squeezed the trigger to the bullet tearing through the flesh of Bates' right upper arm only 0.016 seconds passed. By the time that anyone heard the sound of the gun spitting the bullet out of its muzzle, Bates had been injured for 0.028 seconds.

Of course, the pain had not been registered by Bates by this time. The signal from the bullet hitting the flesh to the brain travels at 0.61 metres a second. The pain signal had to travel 62cm to get to the brain.

A full second after being hit, Bates screamed out in pain, dropping the MCX that he held in his right arm. His trigger arm. Just 1.016 seconds had passed, and one man was effectively out of the fight.

Quinn was already on the move. With Bates out and Woody without ammo, he just needed to take care of Rowland.

He had the MCX raised, the butt of the weapon cradled comfortably in his right shoulder, right hand on the grip, forefinger laid over the trigger guard, left hand under the stock. His right eye looked down the sight while his left, after years of training, managed the peripheral vision.

But the vision was poor. The mask made it difficult to see properly and he did not see Rowland emerge from the van. While he had the weapon focused on the front of NRS van, inside Rowland had opened the rear door and had stepped out onto the platform.

Rowland circled round the van and took aim at the attacker. He hesitated for a second. Was that McEachran? Why was he shooting?

He clocked that Woody wasn't staring at him, but instead his masked face was directed at the rear of the van. He dove for cover behind a steel barrier that was designed to roll behind the shutter door to stop ram raiders. Hitting the ground with a thud, he lost his grip on the rifle and it skidded away out of reach.

He was just in time though. Rowland, seemingly uncaring if it was McEachran or someone else, opened fire. The bullets tore into the metal. The steel was thick. Probably two inches thick. Thankfully, this was enough to protect his prone body from being ripped to shreds.

Quinn looked up and could see Bates cradling his arm, blood dripping off his gloved hands. Woody was stock still in shock and the four captives had all involuntarily dropped to the ground and turned their heads at the sound of the gunfire.

Rowland emptied the full magazine of 30 rounds on fully automatic. The sound in the loading bay was deafening.

As soon as he heard the weapon click empty, Quinn was on his feet again and sprinting towards where Rowland stood. It was a race between him covering the ground between the two of them and Rowland ejecting and replacing the magazine in his weapon.

The loading bay platform was a metre high so he couldn't jump onto it. It was too high. Instead he launched himself headfirst onto the concrete platform, sliding on the dusty ground on his stomach, straight at Rowland.

Rowland fumbled the new magazine and dropped it. Abandoning that action, he grappled for his Glock that sat in a hip holster on his right side. He was too slow.

The momentum of the slide wasn't enough for him to reach Rowland but as he scrambled towards the dirty cop, he drew his knife from its sheath and slammed the blade deep into Rowland' boot. He guessed that he would have reinforced toes in the boot so aimed higher where the knife easily passed through the leather of the boot and wedged itself between the metatarsals.

Rowland screamed out in pain and instinctively lashed out at his attacker. The blow from his balled fist caught Quinn on the back of the shoulder blade. It was an odd place to be punched and certainly not the worst. He stumbled from the momentum of his attack and the subsequent retaliation from Rowland. Regaining his footing he stood and faced Rowland. The injured cop had grasped the handle of the blade and pulled it out his foot, accompanied by a gasp of pain. He mistakenly threw the knife away before looking up at his attacker.

"Who *are* you?" he growled, anger and pain contorting his face under the mask.

He didn't reply, not wanting to risk Rowland recognising his voice. Now unarmed, he raised his fists in answer.

Rowland let out a roar of anger and frustration. "Someone SHOOT HIM!" he yelled.

He glanced back towards where Woody and Bates stood. Woody was lunging for the MCX that hung from Bates' shoulder strap.

He wasn't the only one. Amid the chaos the friends from NRS had shared a look. No words were needed. They each chose the target closest to them and launched themselves at the two men in masks.

Carl attacked Woody from behind, reaching his cable-tied hands over the head of the man who had tried to shoot him just minutes ago. With his linked balled fists clear over the man's head and in front of his throat, he yanked backwards against the forward motion of Woody, the cable ties crushing Woody's larynx, halting his progress and causing him to lose his feet under him. The legs continued forward but the head couldn't follow suit resulting in his feet coming off the ground and in front of him, making him almost horizontal before slamming into the concrete. Carl collapsed on top of him, unable to pull away because of his bound hands.

The wind was knocked out of Woody's lungs and Carl capitalised. He brought his bound and clenched fists down onto Woody's chest as hard as he could almost as if he were trying to restart his heart. He felt a rib crack under the force of his blow.

With Woody gasping for air and clawing at his throat, Carl saw his moment and grappled at the holster on the man's hip and pulled the revolver out of the leather housing. He then scrambled back and aimed the gun at the struggling man he had just attacked. Woody didn't seem to notice. The pain in his chest and the desperate gasps for air was all he could think about.

Marcus had a bigger challenge on his hands. Bates knew how to fight but was injured. The shot wasn't mortal, but it made his right arm mostly useless.

Bates caught Carl's attack out of the corner of his eye and instinctively went for his holstered weapon. The problem was that it was on his right leg and he had to use his left hand. While he fumbled with the leather retaining strap Marcus hit him.

Marcus' shoulder slammed into Bates' ribs where they were exposed from his left arm groping across his torso. The impact sent them both sprawling, Bates crying out in pain as he landed on his injured arm.

They rolled and Bates rose up the quickest. He landed a weak punch to Marcus' face with his uncoordinated left hand. It was enough to send spit and blood from Marcus' mouth.

Again, Bates grappled for his pistol, but Marcus kicked him in the chest sending the dirty cop backwards. Marcus didn't waste any time and followed. He grabbed one of the last bags of cash with both hands. Without breaking stride, he swung the bag with all his might and the bag, full of pound coins, hit Bates on the side of his head. It was like taking a hit from a baseball bat. Bates flew to the ground, briefly unconscious, while the momentum of the weighted swing sent Marcus sprawling too.

The security guard saw his moment and immediately went for the gun holstered on the masked man's leg. Unclipping the retaining strap, he managed to slip the gun out and back away before Bates knew what was going on. Marcus stepped back and joined Carl, aiming the weapon at his antagonist. They nodded a 'well done' to each other before returning their concentration to the two men on the floor.

"You two okay?" Marcus called over his shoulder to Sheila and Graham.

"Y… Yes thanks," they said in unison.

"Good," Marcus acknowledged before quietly asking Carl, "Who's the dude?"

"Got me," Carl replied. "He's got a mask on too though. One of the crew gone bad?"

"Dunno. Ain't that the uniform of the guard at the gate though?"

"Surely not…"

"Fuck," Rowland cursed. "Very well. I'll just have to rip that mask off your face before I shove it down your fucking throat."

Quinn didn't say a word. He just stood there; fists raised. Waiting.

"What, you fucking mute or summet?"

Nothing.

"Well, fuck you then. Here comes the pain sunshine!" With that he too raised his fists and came at him.

Rowland had his guard up in front of his face. He wasn't a brawler. He was a boxer. He knew this from following and researching the bent team. Luckily, Quinn had had a fight or two during his days in the military. He wasn't worried. He should have been.

Rowland came at him with a ferocity that he was not expecting. He came in fast, feet gliding, dancing over the floor. A left jab came flying out and broke through his frail defence with ease. His nose burst and a bloody snotty mixture flew out as his head was knocked back. Momentarily dazed his already weak guard dropped further and another straight jab broke through and caught him in on the cheekbone, the rubber mask threatening to slip.

He reached up and righted the mask while hurriedly taking a few steps back away from the ever-approaching Rowland. *Shit.* He shook his head trying desperately to shake the grogginess away and raised his fists once more.

"You're nothing!" Rowland spat. "I'm gonna crush you!" Again, he attacked.

His feet were so quick, dancing over the ground between to the two men. This time his guard was better, partly blocking the left jabs, one, two… the third found its way through the fists and forearms that tried in vain to protect his face. He reeled from the blow and then, in a blur, a right hook came into view. The mask had affected his peripheral vision and he only saw the viscous right hook as it hit him. Quinn went down, stumbling, his hands splayed, desperately trying to stop his face and body from hitting the dusty concrete. He just managed to find his feet enough to stumble away, retreating from the incensed Rowland.

Rowland screamed. "Get up you fucking faggot. You come in here. You come and fuck with ME?! And this is all you got?"

He turned away from Rowland, confident he was far enough away and raised the mask so he could spit out the blood that was filling his mouth. It was clear that in a straight boxing match, he was not going to win. Hell, he hadn't even thrown a punch. He would have to change it up.

He dropped the mask back down and turned to face his foe, raising his fists once more he went at Rowland. This time he saw the jab coming and ducked to his right, the fist flying millimetres from his face. Once inside the raging man's guard he threw his own right hook, but it just glanced off Rowland's chin, too experienced to fall that. But Rowland was on the back foot so when the kick to his shins came in, he was unbalanced and unprepared.

Rowland cried out in pain. The shin lacks meat to protect the bone. It hurts. So much so that Rowland lost his composure and bent to tend to his shin.

Seeing the angry bent cop bending down, Quinn grabbed Rowland's shoulders, forcing him lower and brought his left knee flying up into his face. He heard and felt his nose snap. *One each* he thought. Rowland reeled away, struggling somewhere between tending to his shin and stemming the blood flowing from his busted nose.

Seeing his moment for redemption Woody launched himself at the distracted NRS man who, along with everyone else, was watching the fight between the two masked men. He went for the one who had stolen Bates' gun. This one he knew was loaded. Marcus saw the movement late and panicking pulled the trigger of the gun. The shot completely missed, and Woody reached him, hands grappling desperately for the weapon.

Then Woody was out cold. Slumped on the floor. Carl had smashed him over the back of the head with the butt of his unloaded gun.

"Cheers bro," Marcus breathed, a little shook up.

"No worries. Now get that loaded weapon facing the other one will ya?"

Their conversation was broken by Graham. "Oh my god! Sheila!"

Both NRS men turned to face the two park employees. Sheila was slumped on the floor, Graham behind her, cradling her head. There was a growing dark red patch on her stomach. The pale blue uniform unable to hide the wet mass.

Graham looked up in desperation and not anger. "You shot her! Shit! You shot her!"

Marcus looked down at his hands and the gun, hastily shoving it into Carls hands. "I...I... I didn't mean to," He stammered. "It was an accident!" He was now pleading.

Carl took the gun and trained it on Bates, but he hadn't moved. "It's gonna be ok, bro. Nobody thinks you did it on purpose. She'll be okay..." He trailed off, looking at Graham for reassurance.

Graham looked down at his bleeding colleague... no, his friend, and said, "I think it's low enough to have missed the major organs, but she needs an ambulance NOW!"

Carl nodded his understanding. Could they help the unknown man? Was he a vigilante? Or was he just another crook? It was hard to tell!

Rowland noticed that the other man had been distracted by the shot ringing out and that gave him the briefest of moments to attack again, ignoring the searing pain in his shin, foot and face. He bundled into the piece of shit who had interrupted his last job. He was gonna make him pay.

He grabbed the man by his throat and pressed his thumbs deep into his windpipe as they both stumbled towards the edge of the raised loading platform. "I've got you now you prick!" he shouted, spit and blood hitting the inside of his mask. But he didn't care. He wanted to break this man!

Rowland pushed harder with his thumbs. Pushed Quinn further back towards the edge. Seething. Spitting. Enraged. But his blind fury was his undoing.

Years of training. Years of working under the cover of night. Years of meditation. He knew not to panic. Knew not lose his shit.

There was always a moment of opportunity. Always that tiny fraction of a second where you could change the outcome. Change the tide. Swing the winds.

He could hear the anger. Taste the rage in the air. The body language was that of a man who was consumed by blinding fury. He could use that. Capitalise. Break free. Break him.

Quinn felt the pressure from the thumbs on his neck just ease off slightly. The edge of the platform was near. Now. The power came from his back, his shoulders and then his arms as he pushed down the arms that were reaching out to his throat. At the same time he dropped his body, all his weight going down through his right leg. He leaned back, using the momentum of Rowland coming at him and the force of his downward movement to propel Rowland up and over his body.

Rowland's grip lessened, the realisation that he was out of control. Flying. Hurtling. Out over the man he thought he had. He was upside down. He had let go of the masked man, unable to hold on. He flailed his arms. Desperate. All he could do was wait. Wait for the impact. He hit the ground, hard. The wind was forced out of his lungs as his body tried to absorb the impact. His head hit the ground, the pain lancing through his nervous system like fire. For the briefest moments he thought he was paralysed until his leg twitched. He was alive but broken. He laid there, staring up at the cobweb surrounded strip lights that hung from the aluminium ceiling. How did it all go so wrong?

Quinn picked himself up and looked down at Rowland. He was out for the count. Broken but alive. He wasn't sure how he felt about that. Pleased he supposed. He never wanted to kill him. Jumping down he then crouched to remove the burnt mask from his face.

Rowland stared up at him, anger and fear clouding his eyes. Rowland spat at him, but it was weak and did not reach its target. He patted him on the chest in an odd reassuring way as if to say, 'It's ok. It's over now.'

From a pocket in his tactical vest he removed some more cable ties. He bound Rowland's ankles and wrists together before casually walking over to the mixed group of NRS workers, Rowland's crew and the two employees. He ignored the gun that wavered in Carl's hand and cable tied Bates and Woody. Satisfied, he covered the four paces to Carl and Marcus. He held out his hands. "Guns please."

Marcus and Carl exchanged looks. Confusion and apprehension written all over their faces. "And you are?" Marcus managed.

"Not one of them," he replied flatly. "Guns," he repeated.

Slowly Carl and then Marcus passed the guns over to him. He shoved both weapons into his waist band. "Thank you, gentlemen. Now please, come with me to the injured woman."

The three of them strode and shuffled over to the bleeding Sheila and the worried Graham.

"How is she?" He asked Graham from behind his mask.

"Bleeding heavily," Graham replied.

"Let me see," he said. It wasn't a question. Graham removed his hands from the wounded area.

He peeled back the shirt to inspect the wound. He tentatively lifted her an inch and slipped his hand behind her back. He pulled out his blood-soaked hand and lowered her back into Grahams arms. "The bullet went straight through. There is a lot of blood loss, but she will be ok," he told them. "Just keep pressure on the wound."

Graham nodded his understanding.

"Sorry boys," he said standing and addressing Marcus and Carl. But I'm going to have to tie you two as well."

The two men looked at each other, confused. Marcus spoke first. "But you're not one of them…"

"No," he admitted. "But I'm not a good guy either." He rested one hand on the butt of one of the Glocks. That was warning enough. Both men held out their wrists, surrendering.

He cable-tied their wrists and ankles just like had done with the others and added. "Good work by the way. Very brave. I'd stay away from guns though, ok?" Both men nodded their agreement.

He looked at the man holding up the injured woman. "Your name?" he asked

"Graham." The park employee replied.

"Ok Graham, I'm not going to tie you up. You need to keep pressure on that wound. You don't, she dies. I'm relying on the fact that you don't want her to die."

Graham looked angry but understood.

"Good."

Chapter 18

Kammy and Smudger sat at a melamine table in a quiet corner of the Cobham motorway services coffee shop. They had bought the G20 van, found a quiet spot near the sea and divvied up the cash. From there they drove in tandem up the A24 through Horsham and joined the M25 at Leatherhead before jumping off at the services. They cradled their cups of coffee in near silence.

Neither man knew what to say. Twenty years of sharing a cell had exhausted almost all of their conversation. Their dreams. Their plans for when they got out. Now, they were on the cusp of the dreams. They had the cash and the time, but here they were, unsure of how to go their separate ways.

Kammy thought about pleading with Smudger one last time but he knew it would be to no avail. The boss was hellbent on taking his revenge and nothing he or anyone else could say was going to change that. Smudger saw it as his destiny. Kammy saw it differently.

But that had all been spoken about and now, here they were, sat in silence like a couple who had mutually agreed that their time together was up, and they were having one last drink before going their own ways. One wanting the split more than the other. Perhaps one having second thoughts, but unable to verbalise them.

"Ready for some sunshine Kammy?" Smudger asked, glancing up from his flat white coffee. He had no idea what a flat white was. When he got locked up there was tea or coffee. Now there more coffee options than there were when buying a new car!

"Always ready to top up the tan!" Kammy said, forcing a grin to spread across his face. "Ready to kill that mothafucka?" He asked, the grin still plastered on his ageing face.

"I'll be honest, Kammy. I'm nervous."

Kammy looked taken aback. He had never heard the boss speak this way. "Nervous?"

"Yeah... not like that! Obviously, I'll fuck him up, but... well, he's been my focus for twenty years! What happens when he's dead? What do I do...?"

Kammy thought he would be speechless, but this was the opening he had been waiting for. "You come find me. We hit some bars. Get laid. Swim in the sea. Buy a boat. A jet ski. Whatever! We *enjoy* life for a while."

Smudger looked unsure.

So Kammy continued. "Then maybe we look up the local gangs, the families who control the island and then we make our move. Take over. Run things our way. *Your way...*"

Smudger grinned. "I like it my old friend. I like it. I'll find you. But for now…"

They tapped their cardboard cups together in a silent toast, finished their drinks and walked off in different directions, their time together done. Two vastly different paths from here on in. One had Bloody Mary's and women. The other just had blood and a man.

Quinn unloaded the Peugeot van into the back of this pickup truck. He hadn't bothered taking any of the cases from the back of the NRS van. He just took the cash that Woody had loaded up. That was more than enough for him. Windsor Great Park was just down the road from the theme park, so he drove the van down to a secluded spot and abandoned it. He then ran the half mile back to his truck, an ambulance on blues the only traffic he saw for which he jumped into a bush to avoid being seen. Someone dressed like him out running at this hour would only attract suspicion.

Sat in his truck, he started the massive V8 hoping that the ambulance was the one he had called for the injured woman. The ever-satisfying rumble reverberated through his now aching body. Stage one complete.

The cops would be here soon as the NRS van had not moved for nearly 45 minutes now. Just as he was about to pull out of the carpark two blue and white's shot up the hill. That was close. He turned left out of the park and headed for Ryan's house.

It was 2am and Millen was borcd, tired and eager to get out and stretch. "That's got to be the last punter now hasn't it?" he asked the others in the apartment.

Norgaard stood at the window, binoculars following the stumbling couple who had just left the club. The woman clung onto the man's arm in a desperate attempt to stay upright and in a straight line. They were loud and jovial. They clearly had nothing to do with what they were looking for.

Evans stood next to Norgaard. "The bouncer closed the door after that couple left so I reckon that it's just staff now."

Millen slurped his coffee and said. "Does that mean we can go now?"

Norgaard lowered the binoculars and turned to look at Millen with contempt. "Of course not. We wait until 4.44. You know that surely?"

"Yeah yeah," Millen dismissed the agent with the stick up his arse. "You two hungry? There's a kebab van round the corner…"

"Sure," Evans replied. "Chicken kebab. Heavy on the chilli sauce. Extra gherkins."

"And you?" Millen asked Norgaard.

"No thank you. I don't eat from Kebab vans."

"You won't last long on a stakeout then mate," Millen scoffed.

"I have my own food thank you." Norgaard pulled a plastic tub from his government issue backpack. Inside he revealed neatly cut white bread sandwiches, an apple, a flapjack and a mini cheese round.

"Fucking hell, mate," Millen laughed. "'Ya mum make you that?" Evans joined him in raucous laughter.

Norgaard looked confused. "Why is that funny? Of course she made it for me."

"Best," Evans heaved. "Thing... I've ever heard!" he managed through gasps of breath and laughter.

They were having much more fun than Tabb and Joseph. The van was beginning to smell funky with the discarded food wrappers and questionable smells emanating from Joseph.

"What time is it?" Tabb asked yawning in the back of the van.

"Half two," Joseph replied from the front seat. "Your turn to keep watch."

"Yeah yeah. Fuck's sake, Joseph. How does your partner put up with you and your smells!?"

"He loves me… and he also farts a lot…"

"Fucking hell. Made for each other."

"I don't know. He still whines a lot!"

They both laughed, changing places so Tabb sat in the front and Joseph took her spot in the back of the van. "Anything happened?" She asked, trying to get comfy.

"Nope. Nextdoor neighbour stood and had a fag outside his front door. The weirdo dog walker did a pass by, but that's it. I've logged it in the book. Wake me before 4.44 or if anyone shows up okay?"

"No worries. Try not to fart in your sleep will ya?"

Joseph let out a yawn. "I'll do my best…"

Quinn parked his truck at the end of Braemer Road where Ryan's house sat, perhaps halfway down. He could see the van that he had spotted the night before. No way that was a coincidence. It could be a new resident, but he doubted it. He was fairly sure that it contained two cops on a stakeout of his brother's house waiting for 4.44. No doubt there by Gilham's instruction.

He waited. The house was ready, and he didn't want to spend any more time in there than he had to.

Smudger pulled into Braemer Road and parked up the van. There were other cars in the road but not many. Most had driveways where nondescript lease-held cars sat. Up ahead he could see a van that was pretty much halfway down the street.

Based on the way the numbers ran, the house he wanted was about halfway down. Glancing at his watch he saw that it was just gone 3am. Nearly time.

He shuffled down in the leather seat and got comfy. This was it. This is what he had been dreaming about for so long now. He ached to see where the family had been killed. Could picture the blood of the filthy cop who had put him away spreading over the floor that was still stained with the blood of his family.

He knew that the house was empty. Knew that he'd been unable to let go, let the house be sold. Unable to move on. Smith liked to think that it was all down to him. That he had been in his thoughts, his dreams… his nightmares for twenty years.

Twenty years of suffering, suffering like he had in that cell. Well, now he was going to live a life he had promised himself and he would end Gabriel Quinn's. End it where his family's blood had flowed.

Smith smiled to himself and gently tapped the sai that lay on the seat next to him. Tonight was to be a good night.

Chapter 19

0434. His watch face illumination was running out of power, but he could just make out the time. Time to move.

Would it be tonight? Would Smith show? He desperately wanted him to. Wanted to bring this to an end. But would it be the end? Smith had ordered the kills but who had carried them out? He had to make Smith tell him. Tell him before he killed him.

He clambered out of the truck and checked he had his knife sheathed and ready. He had left all the guns at the park, clips and ammo removed. He wasn't a gun lover. Good with them, but not a fan.

Being shot was too quick a death for Smith anyway. He had to make him suffer for what he had done. His knife was a last resort. He wanted his hands to do the work. Hands that he had been studying in the pale moonlight since he'd parked here.

He didn't lock the truck, leaving the key stashed under his seat. Nobody on this quiet road at this time was going to nick it. He strode purposefully towards number 38 Braemer Road, noting the van as he passed. He was sure there was someone sat in the driver's seat and wondered who it could be. Millen? Evans? It mattered little.

He marched down the side path and let himself in through the kitchen door, walked to the front door and cracked it open, welcoming Smith should he arrive. Then he sat on the chair that he had positioned himself in the night before in the living room and waited.

Smith looked up, movement in the shadows grabbing his attention. A lone figure was walking purposefully along the road from the opposite direction towards him. Halfway down he turned into a property. That had to be him. Had to be. It was nearly time.

He had indeed figured it all out. 4.44. He was pleased. Pleased that it hadn't been wasted. Pleased that he was definitely going to get what he sought. He opened the door of his van and grasped the sai, locked the door behind him and walked towards number 38, pumped and ready.

"Shit!" Tabb cursed. "Joseph!" she hissed quietly. "Wake up. He's here!"

"Huh?" Joseph replied sleepily pulling himself up off the thin mattress. "Who's here?"

Tabb froze. *Did he just look at me?* The figure walked on and turned into number 38. "Shit!" she cursed again.

"That has to be Quinn. He just walked down the side of the house."

Joseph was now stood behind her. "It's nearly oh forty-four," he said. "Probably is him. Any sign of…" He trailed off as both he and Tabb spotted another figure walking from the other end of the street.

"You think that's Smith?" she whispered.

They both watched in silence as the second man approached number 38 and stood looking at the house. He had something silver and shiny in his hand, the moonlight glinting off its smooth surfaces.

"I'm gonna say it is…"

"What should we do?" Tabb hissed, unmoving.

"Call Gilham. Now."

He heard the front door gently and almost imperceptibly squeak at its hinges. It was being opened. There was no wind this evening; it had to be Smith.

He remained seated, hands calmly placed on each thigh. Relaxed.

He felt the air change somehow. It wasn't a fresh breath of wind, nor a stale and musty draft. More of a change in atmosphere. Colder somehow. Darker.

Then a creak of a floorboard that had always caught Ryan out when returning home late at night.

Then a figure appeared, slowly, tentatively, until the full frame of a man stood at the far end of the living room. Maybe five metres. No, six. It was a long and narrow living room. An odd shape. One that Ryan and Lily had struggled to decide on a suitable layout for. He remembered the conversations; "Where does the tele go?" "Tele?! What about the reading lamp and my aunts Bureau?" Couple stuff.

But now the living room contained the man responsible for the emptiness of this home.

They stared at each other in silence. He could see that Smith held a glimmering silver sai in his right hand. Not unexpected. He couldn't see a bulge that signified a gun either. Perhaps it was stuffed into the belt at the back of his jeans. No matter. Like him it would seem that a gunshot was too quick a death.

Still they just stared in silence, neither man moving… speaking… maybe not even breathing. It was a tense scene even though both men were completely relaxed. Both had dreamt of this moment and they were soaking it all up. Drinking it all in. Savouring it. Eventually he spoke.

"Who did it for you?" Quinn asked, the strain only just showing in his voice.

Smith stared at him, the moonlight reflecting off the mirror over the fireplace. It made the whites of his eyes strangely bright.

"Why should that matter?" Smith replied. "It was I who ordered them to be slain. I orchestrated it all. Told them how it should be done. It is me you should want to kill, to have revenge upon."

"So, there was more than one. Who are they?"

"I told you," Smith was losing his cool, "I am the one. I ordered the kills. It was me who took joy in their deaths. *Me.*" Smith practically spat the last word.

He sensed the anger building in Smith. Sensed that he was under his skin. So easy. He must really want to kill him. "Tell me," he began, "who *killed* them?" His hands involuntarily balled into fists.

Smith let out a roar "I'M GONNA RIP OUT YOUR THROAT!!" Smith lunged across the room at him, the sai tightly gripped in his right hand, forefinger and index finger curled over the central bar of the weapon. Smith was so enraged and lunged with such anger that his movements weren't tight and calculated.

Quinn rose from the chair, grasped the wooden back and thrust it forward, legs facing his attacker. Smith's outstretched right hand containing the sai became entangled in the legs as he twisted the seat. The momentum of the attack was instantly used against Smith, his balance thrown off by the twisting chair. He stumbled harmlessly towards the kitchen door.

Smith quickly regained his composure, spinning and facing Quinn again, snarling. He attacked again. More controlled this time.

Smith came at him with the sai again, but this time in short sharp stabs. He would lunge in, right leg and right arm together. Like a fencer thrusting with their sabre. He darted back, in and out with the rhythm of the lunges, always keeping one eye on the silver weapon. It was like a dance. Choreographed. In and out. In and out.

Then Smith lunged with more power, going from an exploratory jab to a full-on attack. Quinn saw it coming. Saw the muscles tense tighter in Smith's neck before he struck. As the man's arm came close, he swatted it down out of harm's way with his left hand.

Smith's lunge had caused him to lose balance and, as he fell towards him, he thundered his own jab into Smith's face. Flesh on flesh, Bone to bone. A two-inch gash burst open under Smith's left eye causing him to grunt in pain.

He stepped aside to avoid the stumbling, bleeding and angered Smith. He asked again. "Who killed them?" he watched Smith tend to his bleeding face. He saw the fire burning in his blue eyes. Saw the rage erupt at the question. Smith didn't speak this time. He just attacked.

247

Quinn ducked and dived, shuffling around in a desperate effort to avoid the sai that was being thrust with precision now. Smith had channelled the anger. Taken control of it. He grabbed a dust covered cushion off the musty sofa and used it like a shield. The sai ripped into the aged fabric, easily tearing it from the impact point down, polyester stuffing floating like confetti.

Smith came again, jabbing feverishly. He batted the sai away with his left hand, then his right, unavoidably backing away in circles so as not to be pinned against a wall. He had no chance to parry and counter strike. He was up against the ropes.

Quinn didn't see it. He knew it was there but in his hurried movements he misjudged. His left foot dropped back dodging yet another swipe from the sai when his foot hit the coffee table they had been dancing around. He lost his balance, stumbling backwards.

Smith saw his chance and changed tactic. The sai swivelled nimbly in his fingers and he quickly and expertly thrust the weapon down and into the meaty flesh of his right thigh.

He couldn't help it. He cried out in pain, his hands rushing to the spot where he had been impaled.

As quick as it had entered through the flesh it was whipped back out again. He gritted his teeth, not wanting to let on how much pain he was in. Smith knew though. He was grinning at him sickly.

"You see?" Smith sneered, admiring the scarlet blood that trickled down the sai's shaft. "This is how it's meant to be. I. Hurt. You."

He hauled himself to his feet, pain shooting out from the wound, clouding his thought. Again, he gritted his teeth. He needed to disarm him.

But before he could act upon his thoughts, Smith was slashing at him with the weapon. He couldn't move quick enough. The sharpened blade sliced through the skin on his left arm, high up, narrowly avoiding slashing his bicep.

He recoiled in pain, injuries to both sides of his body now. He grappled for anything he could use as a weapon. He still had his knife, but that would not do. Not now.

Quinn's right hand landed on something and he curled his fingers around it. Relief flooding over him. It was a lamp. One of those green glass banker's lamps. *Ryan's.*

He saw the sai this time, slashing through the air, aiming for another blood drawing gash. This time he brought the lamp up to meet the Japanese weapon in a ponderous arc. The green glass smashed against the metal weapon, but the gold curved stand followed through and struck Smith on the hand. He let go of his weapon, grunting with pain.

Unwilling to lose momentum, Quinn swung the lamp again, this time striking Smith in the ribs. He ignored the cries of pain from the wounds Smith had inflicted upon him, intent on hurting his foe. It was Smith's turn to be frantically backing away, dodging the lump of metal that was being wildly swung at him. Smith retreated too much, and he found himself backed up against a wall.

He dropped the lamp and came in at Smith with his fists, delivering blow after to blow to the man's ribs, feeling one snap at last. Smith cried out in pain and anger, throwing himself forward at him. They crashed through the coffee table and across the room, Smith low, protecting his ribs and pushing him backwards.

His backside hit something hard. He grasped a handful of Smith hair and yanked, the man's head coming up quickly, sharp pain and bewilderment filled his eyes. He swivelled, his hand still clutching the man's hair.

Quinn knew what he had backed into. He flipped the lid of the piano and slammed Smiths face down onto the keys, a loud clang of random notes ringing out from the impact. Lily's piano hadn't been played in twenty years. Now it was being abused.

He dragged Smith's face along the keys, pushing his face down as he did so. The room filled with garbled cry's and the tuneless bashing of the old grand piano's keys, blood smeared along the white and black.

Somewhere in his distant consciousness he swore he heard an explosion. He ignored it and, still grasping Smith's hair he yanked up hard and then slammed him against the wall. He changed his grip, this time wrapping one of his huge calloused hands around Smith's neck.

"Tell me who killed my family!" he snarled, spittle flying from his mouth.

Smith struggled, desperately trying to prise his hands off his throat. He gripped harder and Smith's eyes bulged. A slight air of desperation flicked over his eyes. Smith kicked out at him. At anything. He made contact with his shins, but he ignored the pain. His focus was on Smith's face. He wanted answers.

"WHO KILLED THEM!?!" he yelled, his fingers gripping ever tighter around his throat.

Chapter 20

"Holy SHIT!*"* Tabb cried out pointing towards another figure in the dark.

Joseph snapped his head round at the sound, almost dropping the phone in his hand. Tabb could just make out the faint sound of Gilham coming from the tiny speaker.

"What the hell, Tabb?!" Joseph cursed

"Another man!" Tabb gesticulated. "Coming this way!"

Joseph saw him. He was running directly at them. He had something in his hands. *Who was he?!*

Then the figure rolled something under arm straight at them. It bounced awkwardly along the tarmac.

Holy fuck it's a grenade! his mind yelled at him just as Tabb screamed, "GRENADE!!!" Amidst the scrabbling of hands at the handles of the van doors they just heard the muffled cries of Gilham, "GET OUT!!"

It was too late.

The grenade blew right underneath the van. The van in turn exploded, being lifted clean off the ground and into a huge ball of twisted metal and flames. The fuel tank had gone immediately, the fire ripping up the fuel lines, glass blowing outwards in every direction before the van came back down onto the tarmac seconds later.

It was a different van now. No glass. No floor. No survivors.

The lone man did not break his stride. He ran on. Ran into number 38 Braemer Road.

Smith was desperate now and grabbed his wounded arm, but he was focused. Barely noticing his pain receptors pinging his brain with information. "Who did it Smith? WHO DID IT!?"

Then he noticed something change in Smith's eyes. They relaxed and became excited all at once. Then he knew why. He let go of Smith's throat and clawed at his own. A plastic bag or sheet had been thrown over his head, covering his face.

He felt the pull and the pressure on his throat as someone yanked back, pulling him away from Smith. The plastic sucked against his open mouth and nose, suffocating him. He stumbled backwards; his eyes wide with panic.

Calm down, he told himself. *No need to panic.* He saw Smith through the murky plastic coughing and massaging his throat. *Think!* He forced his brain to concentrate. *Idiot.*

Abandoning the desperate attempts to remove the plastic from his throat, he simply straightened his index finger and popped a hole through the plastic and into his open mouth. Air rushed in and he could breath.

Problem one solved. Problem two was whoever was pulling on the plastic. He dug his fingers into the hole he had created and pulled at it, creating a hole large enough for his entire face. Now he could see as well as breath. Smith was looking at him. Smiling.

He felt his legs kicked just behind his knees and he fell, straight onto a chair. *The chair he had used earlier? How did that end up on its feet?* His head was wrenched back by the unknown assailant who still clung onto the plastic that was round his throat.

"You alright, boss?" The voice from behind him said.

Smith's eyes flicked from Quinn to the man behind him. "I am now Kammy. What made you come back?"

"Couldn't let you have all the fun, could I?" he laughed sickly and yanked on the plastic again.

"Well, I'm not gonna lie. Glad to see ya! What was the explosion?"

"Bloody cops wannit? Stakeout van."

"How did you know?"

Kammy just shrugged. "I didn't."

An evil smirk spread across Smith's face as his gaze returned to him. "Your friends are dead and now I have you right where I want you."

Smith swung a punch and connected with Quinn's chin, blood and spit flying out of his mouth as his head twisted to the side. He could hear the two men laughing heartily. He spat blood out onto the floor. Kammy had let go of the plastic around his throat and so he pulled it off over his head and rubbed his chin. Kammy came round and into view. They were obviously confident that their superior numbers meant they had no worries over their captive escaping. They even had the audacity to high five each other.

Smith turned his gaze back onto him. "What shall we do with you now?" He stooped and picked up his sai, turning it over in his hands, noticing the blood with glee. He locked eyes with him and grotesquely licked the blood off the blade. "You taste like the rest of your family did. Weak. Lifeless…"

Quinn lunged out of the chair, everything locked onto Smith and his spiteful words. He didn't see the kick coming from Kammy and took the blow right in the ribs, knocking him off balance and sending him flying across the room. He crashed into the TV cabinet, knocking the old heavy plasma television off and cracking his head on the edge of the unit. *Fuck.*

The two men continued to laugh as he dragged himself to his feet, anger burning in every muscle and tendon. Something caught his eye as he stood. Outside.

The explosion. He could see something on fire.

Oh God. It was the van. Kammy had blown up the surveillance van!

He growled and turned to face the two men once again. "You shouldn't have done that." Every word was dripping with intent.

He went at the men. He hit Kammy first, barrelling his shoulder into his midriff. The two men staggered across the room and through the kitchen door, only stopping when Kammy backed into the worktop. He released himself from Kammy's tangled arms and swung a half uppercut into Kammy's gut, knocking the air out of the murdering bastard.

Doubled over in pain, Kammy didn't see him grasp an old frying pan from the hob and swing it. One clean blow over the back of his head and Kammy slumped to the floor, unconscious and heading for one hell of a headache.

Satisfied that Kammy was out of the fight, he span and went back towards the living room. Smith was stood in the doorway, having followed them to watch the action.

Quinn drew his knife, holding it so the blade ran parallel with his forearm, gritting his teeth in barely contained rage. Smith backed away having seen Kammy go down. Now he was faced with a man who only had eyes for one person. Him. They both raised their weapons. It was on.

Smith took a few paces back before standing his ground, thrusting the sai at his oncoming foe. He parried the jab with his knife, the sound of metal on metal sending a shiver through his body. Smith thrust again, this time he easily parried the attempt and followed through with his own movement, striking Smith in the head with the butt of his knife. Smith was dazed but stood.

He flicked the knife to his left hand and quickly went to punch Smith with his dominant right arm. But Smith saw it coming and slashed with the sai, cutting his arm again. He didn't feel it. He kicked Smith in the knee instead. Smith went down on one knee, crying out.

He reacted quickly, stooping and thrusting the knife deep into the exposed knee of Smith, just below the kneecap. He felt the blade, sleek and sharp on one side and jagged and evil on the other, tear and slice through cartilage, meat, tendons, veins and graze bone on its journey. He did not stop until the hilt of the blade butted against the dirty jeans. The blade had burst out of the rear of Smiths knee, tearing the skin and sending blood spewing out.

Smith screamed. He left the blade burrowed in the knee and stood up, savouring the screams of the man who he hated with all his being. He just watched Smith staring at the blade in his knee, a mixture of agony and bewilderment etched on his tear strewn face. No matter how tough you are, a knife through your knee will reduce you to a whimpering mess of a man.

"Who killed my family?" Quinn asked again with finality. He knew this was the end of Smith's challenge.

Smith didn't reply, shock kicking in. He didn't notice Quinn walk over and grasp the chair he had been sat on earlier. Didn't see him pick up the dropped sai. Didn't see him place the chair next to him. Smith didn't put up any resistance when he grabbed his wrist and placed his hand on the chair.

He knew about it when he screamed out again. Quinn had driven the sai through the palm of his hand, nailing it to the wooden chair. He stepped back again.

"Who killed my family?"

Smith spluttered and moaned in agony, not looking up.

"No more," Smith wheezed. "No more. You win."

"There are no winners here," he replied flatly.

"I wanted to kill you so much. Wanted you to suffer. To pay for the twenty years you robbed from me."

Quinn shook his head, a moment of pity washed over him before he remembered who he was looking at. "Just tell me, Smith."

Smith bowed his head and said quietly through gritted teeth. "I don't know his name. But find a man they call Jansson. He will know."

"Where will I find him?"

"I don't know. Now, please! Call me an ambulance!"

He just shook his head. "Not good enough Smith. He grasped the hilt of the knife roughly and yanked. Hard. Smith screamed louder than he had heard any man scream before. He raised the knife again but stopped when the still screaming Smith held up his remaining hand and shrieked, "Stop!"

He relaxed slightly, his inaction silently telling Smith to continue. He waited for him to catch his breath. His composure.

"Look." Smith struggled to get his words out. "I really don't know who did it. Find Jansson. He's a big Swedish motherfucka. It won't be hard. He runs all the hits round 'ere. Honestly. That's all I know."

He did not know why, but he believed Smith. No man could go through that much pain and not spill all.

"Good enough," he said clearly and darkly. Then he kicked Smith in his savaged knee and repeatedly smashed him in his face with his fists, each blow exorcising a demon deep in his soul. Every wet punch rendered Smith less and less recognisable, his face a bloody pulp. The ex-convict fell unconscious to the ground, his arm awkwardly pulling on the chair where his hand was still impaled. One slash of his knife. That's all it would be, then Smith would be dead. One less cunt in the world. His hand shook. He was loosing blood. He gripped the blade tighter and raised it, ready to strike... Then an overriding flood of emotion hit him. A desire to see one person.

Quinn stood, sheathed his knife and wiped his gloved hands on the t-shirt that Smith wore. He calmly walked to the kitchen and bound the hands of the still unconscious Kammy with a cable tie from his pocket. Satisfied, he marched out of the house and down the road to his truck.

He glanced at the still burning van. Sirens in the distance signalled the imminent arrival of the fire service. Perhaps Charlie Duke would be attending. It was clear that there were no survivors.

He climbed into his truck and started the motor, relishing the roar of the engine. Then he drove away, the carnage behind him.

Chapter 21

"Where the fuck was he?!" Norgaard was apoplectic with rage. He paced Gilham's office, fists clenching and with a face that was as red as Lucifer himself.

It took all of Gilham's considerable composure to not rise out of her chair and scream at the agent. She took a breath and calmly as she could said, "While I understand your frustration, Agent, my more pressing considerations are focused on the fact that I have *two* dead officers. The investigation aside, I have to break this god-awful news to their families. While detective Tabb is not in my force, she was working under my authority and as such it is the least that I could do to inform her family myself. If and when my man surfaces, I am sure that he will be available and willing to answer all your questions. Until that time, can I ask you to refrain from raising your voice in *my* office, respect *my* rank and let *me* do my job?"

Norgaard stopped his pacing and fixed Gilham with a curious glare. "Chief Inspector," he began, ever so slightly calmer than before. "I am truly sorry for the loss of your officers. I am. But can you not see that 'your man' is intrinsically involved here and whether you like it or not, is a suspect in not one but two heinous crimes?" He almost sounded like he was pleading. "Last night thousands of pounds were stolen. Three police officers were caught attempting to steal the money. It is my belief that another, unrelated to them actually stole the money. That same man, I am convinced, inflicted horrendous bodily harm to two other men. That man is missing. I need to interview him."

Gilham sighed. "There is no doubt that Quinn has questions to answer. However, I do not personally think that he is guilty of what you say. Moreover, and I reiterate, he is not my primary concern. Do what you will, but *do not* throw allegations around that you have no substantial evidence to uphold. As soon as I am aware of his whereabouts, I will let you know. Of this you have my word. Until then can I ask for your assistance in sorting through this mess?"

Norgaard's expression softened but the anger was still ablaze in his eyes. "Of course, inspector. What can I do to help?"

"Get to the hospital. Question Rowland. Find out what he knows about the man who foiled him. We now have a confession from my secretary who had been, unbeknownst to me, dating Rowland. She told him about the money at the court."

Norgaard looked as though he was about to argue but thought better of it. He simply nodded acknowledgement and said, "Ma'am," before leaving the office, shutting the door firmly without slamming it.

Gilham slumped back in her chair, exhaled deeply and whispered, "Where are you?!"

Millen and Evans were en route to the hospital, tired and thoroughly devastated. Not only had they lost colleagues, but they hadn't been there to help. They had been at the wrong location watching a bar that was for all purposes completely unrelated.

They were also suffering from guilt. It was of course not their fault, but they hated themselves, nonetheless.

Their task was to interview Smith. From what they heard he had some horrendous injuries. Whoever it was that inflicted them, they had done a good job.

Could it have been Quinn? Everything pointed to the one suspect, of which they had no idea of his whereabouts. If it were him, they were glad, in amongst the sadness, anger and guilt, that he had had some kind of cathartic experience. But had he got what he wanted? Why hadn't he killed Smith? They both felt that had they been in his shoes they would have almost certainly killed him.

"Reckon he'll talk?" Millen asked his partner who was staring at the road ahead.

Evans glanced across at his long-time friend. "Not a chance," he said glumly. "But we'll have to try."

Millen looked away and asked. "Joseph had a partner, didn't he?"

"Yup."

"Fuck. I wouldn't want to be in Gilham's shoes right now."

"No fucking way," Evans admitted, taking a left into the Royal Berkshire Hospital car park. He pulled into a visitor space and shut off the hybrid vehicle. "Shall we?" He asked rhetorically. Both men silently exited the vehicle and headed off to interview one of the worst criminals they had ever come across.

He had been a key part in a night of absolute carnage. He had wounds. He was beaten but he was successful. He had driven his truck back to the lockup and stashed the cash in his safe. He knew that he was never going to be able to deny the actions at Ryan's house. How could he? It would not take long for even the most incompetent detective to work out that it was him. He didn't have anything to hide. It was self-defence. Simple.

What he could not afford to be pinged for was anything to do with Rowland and his crew. That was made slightly harder by the fact that he had evidence on his thumb drive of the robbery at the county court. It was going to look highly suspicious and he suspected that was what the man in Gilham's office was there for.

He'd looked him up. His name was Norgaard. MI5. But this wouldn't be the first time that this had happened and clearly why Norgaard was in. Having said that, there was nothing that he knew of that directly tied him or placed him at the scene – at least nothing that would show his face. He had planned on mounting a camera to capture the fight with Rowland but had soon realised there was CCTV so relied on that footage. He had not shown his face. Of this he was confident.

He would have to go to the station at some point. He figured that he might as well go now and make the most of the medical team on site to get cleaned up. Some of the wounds he knew would need stitches.

He changed clothes into some jeans, a plain grey T-shirt and tentatively pulled a maroon hoodie over his head, wincing at the pain. Lastly, he picked up the thumb drive and left the lockup. "Here goes," he said into the crisp morning air.

Epilogue

Two weeks had passed, and the wounds were healing. At least the physical ones were. The closure that he had sought… expected, had not come to pass. Smith was done. Smith was finished, but the real killer or killers perhaps were still out there and all he had was a name.

Jansson.

Who were they? Was it even a he?

He couldn't focus on it now. Too much had passed and he needed a rest. He had been grilled for days about his whereabouts on that fateful night. Norgaard had been desperate to pin the theme park job on him. When the thumb drives had made an appearance, the stockpile of cash had been recovered. That had taken some of the heat off him, but still Norgaard came for him.

He had been careful. He wasn't a rookie at this shit. His tracks were covered. In the end there was nothing Norgaard could pin on him. This time. He would have to be even more careful in the future.

Then there was the deaths of Joseph and Tabb. That had hit him and the force hard. It seemed to be taking a massive toll on Gilham. She seemed to be taking it too personally.

He understood. Sympathised even, but it was a risk of the job. She hadn't killed them, and they had the man that did. Kamara and Smith were going away for a long time, that much was for sure. They had both accused him of being the one who had beaten them. There was no denying that, but Gilham had pulled in some favours and, for this time at least, he wasn't in the firing line. The trauma of the last twenty years clearly sat badly with some within the force and he had been covered for.

Gilham had come forward as his alibi for the evening. He owed her his life.

The woman from the park had recovered from her gunshot wound and Rowland's crew were in for a very long trial followed by a quite frankly torrid time behind bars. Cops in prison? It was never going to be easy, but that was of no concern to him. He had done his job.

The quiet seaside village of Wittering passed him by as he drove through, deep in reflective thought, his driving in autopilot. His car boot was laden with cash and as he pulled into the long drive of Lionel House he returned to the present, noting the overgrown wisteria that set the grounds in shade from the late sunshine.

The gravel crunched under his feet on his way to the front door, turning to silence when he crossed onto the paved entranceway to the grand old house.

You would never have suspected that this property would hide sophisticated security systems. He lent down and let the retina scanner read his left eye. The system, satisfied that it was him then prompted a hand scan on the glass screen that popped out from the faux brick wall.

The technology made a faint beep of acceptance and he heard the mechanical clunk of the door locks releasing. The door swung open slightly inviting him in. He pushed it wide open and stepped across the threshold.

The house looked abandoned but inside it was clinically clean. Shutting the door firmly behind him and clutching the army green duffel bag he called out. "Hello?"

Silence greeted him briefly before he heard footsteps on the old wooden stairs. A woman in pale green nurses' scrubs came into view. Cassie was in her mid-twenties and had been working for him for the last two years. Before her it had been her mother, Lucille, and together they had served him well. They were well paid for sure, but they cared, and they were discreet. Those two things were worth more to him than any money.

Cassie smiled in greeting and said cheerily. "So nice to see you Gabriel! It has been a while."

"I'm sorry," he replied "It really has been full on recently. I have your money," he said as way of apology, holding up the duffel bag.

She gave him an odd look, understanding his hesitancy. "Great," she said warmly. "Leave it there and come on up. She's doing really well."

He left the bag in the foyer and followed Cassie up the stairs, desperately trying to avoid looking at her pert backside. *Too young!* He chastised himself.

They made their way down the short corridor and tuned left into one of the bedrooms. One of only two that were used.

He paused briefly at the doorway, unsure if he should really enter. Cassie sensed his indecision and beckoned him in with a smile. He stepped into the bright coloured room and noted the fresh flowers on the bedside table.

The familiar and haunting sound of the ventilator greeted him, and he closed his eyes briefly willing the sound to go away.

When he reopened them all the familiar feelings of guilt, sadness and terror flooded over him. There, neatly tucked up in the large double bed lay Lily. Serene and beautiful and in a coma.

In that moment Gabriel Quinn was reminded why he did what he did. Why he broke the very laws he upheld…

Hope and love.

Printed in Great Britain
by Amazon